Unexpectedly, Hitler smiled.

'Operation Hercules will take place in mid July, gentlemen,' he said decisively. 'In the meantime, Kesselring, II Air Corps is to maintain heavy attacks on the island and the ships endeavouring to supply it. I want every installation on Malta pounded to dust; I want the people dazed and broken, cowering in their caves like animals, so that when we do come they will throw themselves at our feet and beg for mercy.

'You will no doubt have heard,' the Führer concluded, 'that two weeks ago the British awarded the island of Malta their highest civil decoration, the George Cross, in recognition of what they termed the people's bravery in withstanding our air onslaught.

'I want you to make it clear to them, Kesselring, that the onslaught is only just beginning.'

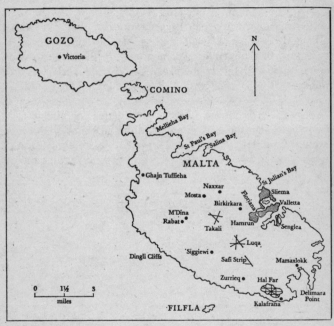

Map of Malta and Gozo in 1942

MALTA VICTORY

Yeoman on the George Cross Island

ROBERT JACKSON

CORGI BOOKS

A DIVISION OF TRANSWORLD PUBLISHERS LTD

MALTA VICTORY
A CORGI BOOK 0 552 11856 7

Originally published in Great Britain
by Arthur Barker Ltd.

PRINTING HISTORY
Arthur Barker edition published 1980
Corgi edition published 1981

This book is set in 10 pt. Times Roman

Corgi Books are published by Transworld Publishers Ltd.,
Century House, 61–63 Uxbridge Road,
Ealing, London, W5 5SA

Made and printed in the United States of America by
Offset Paperbacks, Dallas, Pennsylvania.

Chapter One

It had been raining for two days, and although the sky was now clear except for a few freckles of high cloud the pine-woods still dripped with moisture. Drops fell from the branches and spattered the bonnet and windscreen of the gleaming Mercedes staff car that slid along the narrow road at a steady twenty kilometres per hour; a higher speed was strictly forbidden.

The two occupants of the back seat both wore Luftwaffe uniform. One of them, a sinewy, sunburned man with the rank of general, whose uniform sported paratroop insignia, turned suddenly and glanced through the tinted, bullet-proof rear window. Behind the staff car came two BMW R75 motor-cycle combinations, the helmeted soldiers in the side-cars huddled purposefully behind MG-34 machine-guns.

The general smiled to himself, and gave his companion a sidelong look. 'I see they're taking no chances, as usual Herr Feldmarschall,' he murmured.

The other made no reply. Privately, he thought: one gets used to the security, to the armed escorts, to the cold, impersonal inspections by ss guards that were an inescapable feature of every visit to the Wolfschanze, Adolf Hitler's 'Wolf's Lair' at Rastenburg in East Prussia, set in its gloomy, damp woods.

There were no exceptions. Even the Führer's closest friends were subjected to the same procedure. Yet there was no escaping the calculating logic behind it all; sometimes, one's friends were the people one had cause to fear most.

The Wolfschanze was a far from easy place to get into, and just as hard to get out of. The defensive perimeter that ran through the woods was built in three rings, each protected by minefields, pillboxes and electrified barbed-wire fences. Each ring was patrolled day and night by ss troops, all armed to the teeth and accompanied by savage Dobermann guard dogs. These were trained to attack and kill on a single command from their masters; they were not trained to respond to any attempt to call them off.

The Mercedes and its escorts reached the last of the three defensive rings, the one surrounding the inner compound with its complex of buildings that made up Hitler's headquarters, and drew to a stop. A heavy machine-gun mounted on a tower swivelled towards it as soldiers swung open the massive double gate that barred its way and motioned to the driver to pull over beside a low concrete building that served both as guardhouse and security police HQ.

One of the officers in the car, the senior of the two, drummed his fingertips impatiently on the leather upholstery of the seat. It was always like this, he reflected. They always kept one waiting for at least five minutes at this point, as if to emphasize who the real bosses were.

This time, however, the wait was slightly less. After only three minutes, a man in a black uniform and gleaming jackboots emerged from the police building. The occupants of the car recognized him at once as Oberführer Rattenhuber, commander of the ss Guard and ss Reichsführer Heinrich Himmler's chief of security. Rattenhuber, one of his deputies, always gave visitors to the Wolfschanze a personal scrutiny before allowing them to proceed into the inner sanctum.

These particular visitors were already well known to the ss Oberführer; nevertheless, he peered intently at them through the open side window of the Mercedes and took a long time over examining their special passes as well as their personal identity cards. The passes were valid for one visit only, and had to be surrendered on the way out at the last checkpoint.

As a matter of fact, Rattenhuber wasn't paying much attention to the identity documents at all. He liked to keep right up to date not only with the conduct of the war, as seen from the vantage-point of the Führer's headquarters, but also with the men responsible for waging it. Rattenhuber and his personal staff knew the whereabouts of every officer in the German Army and Air Force, from the rank of colonel upwards; the smaller fry were someone else's business, and so was the Navy. Admiral Canaris, Head of Intelligence, insisted on the ss having nothing to do with the Navy, and one day, Rattenhuber thought grimly, Canaris was going to come a cropper.

So Rattenhuber pretended to scrutinize the documents in minute detail, while his brain worked overtime. Something big, he thought, must be brewing in the Mediterranean, for these two to be summoned here at the same time. It had to be the Mediterranean, because Field-Marshal Albert Kesselring, one of the men who sat twitching with impatience in the staff car, had been withdrawn with his entire staff from the central sector of the Russian front and designated Commander-in-Chief South, with his headquarters at Messina in Sicily, and now controlled all the Luftwaffe units in that part of the world.

Then there was the man who sat next to Kesselring, General Kurt Student, paratroop commander of the XI Air Corps, who had lost half his men in the invasion of Crete a year ago, in May 1941. The paratroops hadn't been doing much since then; in fact they hadn't been doing anything at all in the way of their proper job, being used as infantry units in Russia instead.

So, mused Rattenhuber, you put Kesselring and Student together, and what do you get? An airborne landing somewhere in the Mediterranean, that's what. And, he thought, I'll bet I know where. Cyprus. They'll take off from Crete and drop on Cyprus. What a masterstroke! With Cyprus in the bag, we'll be able to invade Palestine and then march on

Egypt to link up with General Rommel's Afrika Korps from the opposite direction.

All these thoughts went through Rattenhuber's mind in a matter of seconds. Yet again, he prided himself on his excellent grasp of military strategy. Why, it was almost as astute as the Führer's. Positively glowing with self-satisfaction, he handed the passes back to the men in the car with a flourish, snapped to attention with a Nazi salute, and waved the vehicle on.

Kurt Student let his breath escape in a long, exasperated explosion as the car drew away. These SS swine, he told himself, were fast becoming a state within a state, possessing almost unlimited power. One day, it would be the Wehrmacht's duty to crush the lice. He was still fuming when the driver brought the Mercedes to a halt.

SS orderlies, standing stiffly to attention, held the car doors open and the two officers got out, inhaling the fresh scent of the pine-woods that came to them on a light breeze. The Mercedes had stopped in front of a low, wooden building over which the Nazi swastika flew; apart from that, it was completely unadorned. This was the Lagebaracke, the place where Hitler held his daily military conferences.

They were greeted formally by an SS Sturmbannführer —the equivalent of a lieutenant-colonel in the Wehrmacht, but possessing considerably more power and influence—who showed them into an anteroom and asked them with unexpected courtesy, if they wished for coffee. Both men declined. Student glanced at his watch; it was 11.30 a.m. Their meeting with the Führer was due to take place in fifteen minutes' time. Student wondered who else would be present: certainly not the usual cluster of generals and field-marshals, for Hitler's main staff conferences were held in the afternoon.

At 11.45 on the dot, the paratroop general's curiosity was satisfied. Carrying their briefcases, he and Kesselring were ushered along the short corridor that led to the conference room. The door was open, and as they entered both slammed to attention and gave the Nazi salute, right arms outstretched.

Normally, both men would have given the ordinary Wehrmacht salute, but to do so on this occasion would not have been favourably received by the man who faced them across the heavy oak table that dominated the room.

Adolf Hitler, wearing his favourite light grey tunic and dark trousers, nodded affably at the two officers and motioned to them to join him on his side of the table. He shook hands with both of them, and when he spoke his voice was soft, almost melodious, with none of the harsh overtones that characterized his Party speeches. For a minute or two he made small talk, enquiring after their health, and passed a few remarks on how the war on the Eastern Front was progressing. The Wehrmacht had opened a new offensive and was pushing on towards the Caucasian oilfields, with one army crossing the Don to thrust between the Black Sea and the Caspian and another advancing towards the Volga, where its objective was a city named Stalingrad. In North Africa, too, the situation was highly auspicious, with General Rommel on the point of launching another major offensive.

While appearing to hang on Hitler's every word, Student glanced covertly around the room. There was only one other occupant, a stenographer. Several windows permitted a view of the pine-trees beyond the fringe of the compound. Two or three were open and a breeze wafted into the room, lifting a corner of the large map which was spread over the table. The general's eyes fixed on a wall calendar; the date it showed was 30 April, 1942. Someone had forgotten to alter it, for today was the first of May.

Suddenly, Hitler's voice took on an incisive quality and he slapped the map with the palm of his hand.

'Well, gentlemen, to business. Operation Hercules. Kesselring, your report, if you please.'

Field-Marshal Kesselring cleared his throat and looked at the Führer, meeting the latter's piercing gaze directly.

'Mein Führer,' he began, 'since I last reported verbally to you our air operations against the island of Malta have been greatly intensified. Up to the beginning of March, we were sending out our bombers in small numbers to make precision attacks on selected targets. I subsequently became convinced that such a course of action led only to too much diversification of effort, and decided that the real solution lay in using all our bombers as one unified force for large-scale attacks.'

Student raised an eyebrow. That decision had been reached some time ago by Colonel Paul Deichmann, Chief of Staff of II Air Corps, and it was only recently that Kesselring had agreed to implement it.

'Our revised plan,' Kesselring went on, 'encompassed a threefold task. The first priority was to knock out the British Air Force's principal fighter base on Malta, that is to say Takali airfield; next to attack the bomber and torpedo-bomber bases of Luqa, Hal Far and Kalafrana; and, thirdly, to destroy the dock and harbour facilities of the Valletta naval base.'

The Field-Marshal paused and glanced down at a report he had taken from his briefcase. Then he continued:

'The first major attack on Takali was carried out at dusk on 20 March, and we followed it up with a second maximum-effort raid the next day. In both cases, we were able to mount some two hundred sorties over the island. The effort was maintained almost non-stop over the next five weeks, and, if the Führer desires, he may gauge the result from the figures contained in II Air Corps' latest situation report.'

Kesselring handed a sheet of paper to Hitler, who peered at it short-sightedly. Classified *'Streng Geheim'*—Top Secret —it was dated 28 April. 'During the period 20 March until 28 April 1942,' it read, 'the naval and air bases of Malta were completely put out of action. In the course of 5,807 sorties by bombers, 5,667 by fighters and 345 by reconnaissance aircraft, 6,557,231 kilograms of bombs were dropped. Our air reconnaissance indicates that only twenty Spitfires and Hurricanes remain serviceable on the entire island . . .'

'Six and a half million kilos of bombs,' Hitler mused. He looked up at Kesselring. 'That is almost as much as we dropped on England in August and September 1940, is it not? And still this mound of dirt in the Mediterranean continues to survive.'

Kesselring nodded. 'But not for much longer, mein Führer. Our bombers have destroyed almost every transport attempting to run supplies through to the island, and reports from our agents indicate that the population is starving. More important, the third phase of our offensive, against the British naval bases on Malta, was highly successful. Their destroyers and submarines have been driven away, as have the bombers of the Royal Air Force. The supply convoys for the Afrika Korps can now cross the Mediterranean to Tripoli and Benghazi without being molested.'

Hitler's gaze switched suddenly to Student. 'General,' he said, 'how are the preparations of XI Air Corps progressing? Report, please.'

Student phrased his sentences carefully, conscious of Hitler's eyes boring into him and aware of what was passing through the Führer's mind. Whenever airborne operations were proposed these days, the shadow of Crete and the heavy losses sustained during that operation always lurked in the background. Somehow, Hitler had to be convinced that Operation Hercules, the airborne invasion of Malta, could and would succeed.

The paratroop general spoke quietly, and with no embellishment. 'Mein Führer,' he said, 'Operation Hercules has now been in the throes of preparation since last December, and our intelligence on the enemy's defensive positions is excellent. We have information on every flak emplacement, every machine-gun post. We have prepared models of every fortified point; we know the calibre of the weapons that defend them, and their field of fire.'

He paused to let the words sink in. Hitler looked at him without expression, and he went on:

'As the Führer is aware, the operation will be a joint German-Italian venture and will be under the command of Marshal Count Cavallero. I have the utmost confidence in his ability. He has a total of thirty thousand men at his disposal, a number equal to the entire British garrison. Besides my own XI Air Corps, the force includes the Italian paratroop division "Folgore", which was trained by my friend and colleague Major-General Bernhard Ramcke, and the glider-borne Division "Superba". Ramcke reports that he is very impressed by "Folgore's" standard of efficiency. In addition, six Italian divisions totalling seventy thousand men are ready to carry out a seaborne invasion in the wake of the airborne assault. All in all, the force is six times stronger than the one we assembled for the operation against Crete.'

'And aircraft?' Hitler interjected impatiently, as though wishing to make the conference as brief as possible. 'How many aircraft has Conrad assembled for Hercules?' Major-General Conrad had been responsible for the armada of transport aircraft and gliders which had carried out the air-drop on Crete the previous year; now he was faced with an even greater task.

'In this respect also,' Student continued unhurriedly, 'we are very well situated. Conrad has been allocated ten groups, totalling five hundred Junkers 52 transports, and since their bases are less than one hundred and twenty kilometres from Malta they should be able to make four round trips during the first day of the invasion. As far as gliders are concerned, there are three hundred DFS 230s, the same type that we used in the Cretan operation, and two hundred Gotha 242s. The former can carry ten fully-equipped men, the latter twenty-five. In the glider operation alone, therefore, we can put eight thousand men into the combat zone in one drop. The gliders, of course, will go in first immediately after the air bombardment. The first wave will consist of DFS 230s, which will use their special parachutes to make—'

'Special parachutes?' Hitler interrupted. 'What special parachutes? Be good enough to explain.'

'Two hundred of the 230s,' Student informed him, 'have been fitted with special braking parachutes. These are deployed just before touchdown, enabling the glider pilots to make very short and precise landings close to key points such as flak positions, command centres and some rather mysterious caves our reconnaissance aircraft have detected. We do not know exactly what is inside them, but we think they are dumps for fuel and ammunition. Immediately after the glider assault, six Junkers 52 groups will drop their paratroops over selected targets on the island, one of which is the airfield of Luqa. Once this is in our hands, four more Ju 52 groups will land there with the remainder of the airborne force.'

Student fell silent, and now Kesselring spoke again.

'Mein Führer,' he said, 'Operation Hercules cannot possibly fail. Malta is even now within our grasp. Our bombers will sweep the seas around the island, preventing the British Fleet from interfering with our seaborne invasion force. The island is starved of supplies of every kind, its will to resist seriously undermined. We must strike soon.'

Hitler stared at him for a moment, then gazed at the map on the table, his long fingers toying with a pencil. After a minute or two he crossed to one of the windows and stood with his hands behind his back, taking deep breaths of the pine-fresh air. Then, abruptly, he swung round on his heel and faced the two officers.

'Gentlemen,' he said, 'I wish it were as simple as that. In fact, it is not. In the Libyan desert, General Rommel reports that the British Eighth Army is making preparations for a new offensive at Gazala. Rommel must attack with Panzerarmee Afrika before the British offensive has time to develop, and he must do it soon.' The Führer smiled briefly.

'Thanks to the efforts of your bombers, Kesselring, Rommel now has sufficient supplies of ammunition and fuel to last four weeks. He is confident that in that time he can smash through the British defences at Gazala, capture Tobruk and drive on to the Egyptian frontier.

'I have to tell you, gentlemen,' Hitler continued, 'that three days ago I reached agreement with Mussolini on the order of priority. First, in June, Tobruk must be captured. Then, in July, we will turn our attention to Malta. Besides, Kesselring, the Duce does not share your belief that Operation Hercules cannot fail. He expressed the opinion to me that the preparations have been too hasty, that too much has been left to chance. He wishes for more time, for further air attacks on Malta.'

The Führer gave a sudden snort, and rubbed the tip of his

nose with his index finger. 'No matter what Major-General Ramcke thinks about the efficiency of the Duce's airborne troops, gentlemen, you both know my views on the combat capabilities of our allies,' he grunted. 'If the invasion of Malta were to go ahead immediately, there is no doubt that the British fleet at Gibraltar and Alexandria would try to intervene, regardless of cost. And suppose your bombers were unable to operate for some reason, Kesselring? Suppose the British Navy got through to intercept the seaborne invasion force? The whole lot, Italian warships and all, would turn tail and run for it, leaving Student's paratroopers sitting on Malta in splendid isolation.'

Kesselring began to protest, but Hitler held up his hand to silence him. 'No, Kesselring, I will hear no objection. For once I agree with the Duce. We need more time. The British Army in North Africa must be destroyed, the British Fleet in the Mediterranean must be shattered by air attack before we can contemplate an invasion of Malta. There must be no repetition of the disastrous losses your men sustained in Crete, Student. Even now, I shudder to think what might have happened had our bombers not been in a position to keep the Royal Navy at bay.'

He glared at Student, and the latter winced. Then, unexpectedly, Hitler smiled.

'Operation Hercules will take place in mid July, gentlemen,' he said decisively. 'In the meantime, Kesselring, II Air Corps is to maintain heavy attacks on the island and the ships endeavouring to supply it. I want every installation on Malta pounded to dust; I want the people dazed and broken, cowering in their caves like animals, so that when we do come they will throw themselves at our feet and beg for mercy.

'You will no doubt have heard,' the Führer concluded, 'that two weeks ago the British awarded the island of Malta their highest civil decoration, the George Cross, in recognition of what they termed the people's bravery in withstanding our air onslaught.

'I want you to make it clear to them, Kesselring, that the onslaught is only just beginning.'

Chapter Two

The big hangar deck of the American aircraft carrier USS
Wasp was a shuddering, vibrating cavern of noise. The ship
had turned into wind and tremors buffeted her hull as she
ploughed into the swell at full speed, her engines pounding.

Strapped tightly in the cockpit of his Spitfire, Flight
Lieutenant George Yeoman glanced up at the great black
girders that stretched up into the gloom on both sides, beyond
the green, spectral glow of the hangar's electric lights, then
looked around him as far as the restriction of his seat harness
would permit. The hangar deck was choked with Spitfires,
packed nose to tail, wingtip to wingtip, like a school of fish
swept into the belly of a leviathan. There were thirty-six of
them, and Yeoman knew that another thirty or so were
crammed on the flight deck of the British carrier HMS *Eagle*,
churning through the sea not far away.

Yeoman was suddenly conscious of the date: 9 May, 1942.
It was two years, all but a day, since he had first gone into
action in France as a very new sergeant pilot, flying Hurricanes with No. 505 Squadron while the British Expeditionary
Force carried out its famous fighting retreat to Dunkirk. A lot
had happened to him since then; the Battle of Britain, the
Western Desert, Crete. Now he was an old hand at the age of
twenty-two, with the ribbons of the DFC and DFM on his chest
and thirteen confirmed victories to his credit.

Somewhere behind him a Merlin engine coughed into life
and a wraith of blue exhaust smoke drifted slowly over his

head. He looked in his rear-view mirror and saw American sailors seize a Spitfire by its wingtips, pushing it backwards on to the big hangar lift by the side of the ship. The seamen ran clear, carefully avoiding the shimmering arc of the Spitfire's propeller, and the lift disappeared smoothly up into the shadows. Seconds later it descended once more, empty. Somewhere over Yeoman's head the sound of the Merlin rose to a shrill crescendo, then faded as the Spitfire roared away from the flight deck.

More engines started, and another Spitfire was dragged on to the lift. The hangar deck was partly open to the outside, which made it possible to start engines down here in relative safety. The procedure was impossible on British carriers, with their enclosed hangar decks, where the slightest spark could ignite explosive petrol fumes and tear the ship apart.

The American procedure certainly saved time and congestion on the flight deck, thought Yeoman, as the empty lift came down again and the fighter it had carried winged out over the sea. He glanced at his watch; it was 5.20 a.m. and outside the sun was just beginning to rise. He was still quite a long way down the queue, with seven or eight Spitfires to go before him.

He looked across at the fighter on his left and grinned at its pilot, who stuck two fingers up at him. Yeoman made a mental note to pay Flying Officer Gerry Powell the two pounds he owed him as soon as they reached their destination; there had been an almost non-stop poker school in progress on the *Wasp* ever since she had left the Clyde and Yeoman, who was by no means an expert at the game, had a fair-sized hole in his pocket as a result.

He liked Powell. The pint-sized Canadian had an irrepressible sense of humour and by all accounts was a first-rate pilot with half a dozen Huns to his credit. He had fallen out with somebody somewhere along the line, however, hence his current posting. It was the same with many of the other pilots on the two carriers; they were a pretty wild bunch, all told, and their previous commanding officers had apparently been pleased to see the back of them. But there was no denying one fact: they were tough and determined, and when they were let off the leash they were killers. Their operational records and the medal ribbons they wore testified to that fact.

As far as Yeoman was concerned, the task ahead of him was infinitely preferable to his last job. In December 1941, at the end of his time in the Middle East, he had returned to the United Kingdom for a 'rest' as a flying instructor, and hated every minute of it. Some people enjoyed the task, but flogging round an aerodrome circuit day in, day out, had proved more soul-destroying than Yeoman had ever imagined. Either a pilot was cut out to instruct, Yeoman had quickly concluded, or he wasn't. His fellow instructors had been a pretty morose bunch, too, which had not helped matters, but even that would not have been so bad if it had not been for the CO of the training school, a man with whom Yeoman had found it impossible to get on at all. Both had taken an instinctive dislike to one another at first sight, and it seemed to Yeoman that from then on his superior had gone out of his way to make life uncomfortable for him.

He didn't know what sort of chip lay across the man's shoulder, and he didn't care. All he knew, after two months, was that unless something drastic happened to change things he was going to blow his top, and to hell with the consequences.

Then, in April, a chance to escape from the tense, unhappy atmosphere of the flying school had fallen into Yeoman's lap, and he had seized it eagerly. Another instructor, a flight lieutenant named Gill—who, for some reason, was one of the CO's blue-eyed boys—had looked so down in the mouth over breakfast one morning that Yeoman had asked him what was wrong. Gill, it turned out, was bewailing the fact that he had just been warned of a posting overseas. Yeoman had listened patiently to the man's tirade; he had only been married three months, his wife was expecting a child, it wasn't fair to send him of all people abroad just at this time, and so on.

Ordinarily, Yeoman wouldn't have given a damn about Gill's fate. His Majesty paid you to take whatever was coming to you, and that was that. But this was different. He had leaned over the table and quietly asked Gill if he could go in his place. For a moment, the other had stared at him in stunned silence; then he had seized his hand and pumped it in an embarrassing show of emotion.

Half an hour later Yeoman had been in the CO's office, making a formal application to swap places with Gill. The CO had been in an unexpectedly genial mood, and had promised to fix everything. He had been as good as his word; indeed, Yeoman had left the office with the clear feeling that if the man had been faced with the prospect of paying the young pilot's fare to his unknown overseas destination, he would have done so willingly.

Seven days later Yeoman, bowed under the weight of his personal kit, parachute pack, dinghy pack, Mac West life-jacket and the other odds and ends essential to his profession, had reported to the Rail Transport Officer on Glasgow Central station, to find that thirty-five other pilots were converging on the same spot from all points of the compass. None of them knew the nature of their destination, but they had all been told that they would have to take off from an aircraft carrier and consequently there had been a lot of rumours. Some had thought they were heading for north Russia, where a couple of RAF Hurricane squadrons had been operating alongside the Soviet Air Force for some months, but Libya was the favourite choice.

They had joined the USS *Wasp* that night, and she had sailed from the River Clyde before dawn, pointing her bow southwards into the Atlantic. Only then, at a briefing the following morning, did they learn the facts. They were to be the reinforcements the besieged island of Malta needed so desperately.

Yeoman would always remember that briefing. It was given by the senior RAF officer, Squadron Leader Roger Graham, who would command the pilots on the *Wasp* until they landed on the island. They would then be split up and assigned to the various airfields; Graham himself was to command a squadron at Luqa.

Graham had been in Malta before, the previous spring.

19

The story he told the assembled pilots, simply and without elaboration, was one of fearful privation and enormous courage. He told them how Malta, the key strategic position in the central Mediterranean, had been isolated by Italy's entry into the war on the side of the Axis in June, 1940, and how the island had been subjected to an almost continual onslaught from the air ever since by the Italian Air Force and the Luftwaffe. He spoke of the early days of the battle, when Malta had been defended solely by three old Gloster Gladiator biplanes. Then a trickle of Hawker Hurricanes had started to arrive, and they had sustained the air defences, fighting against appalling odds, until June 1941, when the Luftwaffe units in Sicily had been withdrawn for operations on the Russian front and left the Italians to continue the offensive on their own.

The Luftwaffe's absence, however, had been only temporary. In December 1941 the bombers returned, and over the next three months they unleashed a series of attacks whose fury made the previous raids seem almost insignificant. By the end of February, the island's force of sixty Hurricanes had been halved, the survivors faced with the impossible task of taking on the two hundred and fifty bombers and two hundred fighters the enemy had assembled on Sicily.

In a desperate attempt to alleviate the situation, the carrier HMS *Eagle* flew off fifteen Spitfires on 7 March, and these joined the Hurricanes in three weeks of hectic air fighting. By the end of the month, however, there were only eighteen serviceable fighters on the whole of the island, and only Luqa airfield was still operational. The RAF's small bomber force, and the Royal Navy's warships—both of which had taken a fearful toll of Rommel's supply convoys—were forced to leave. Malta was being systematically torn apart, and although the courage of the islanders remained unbroken, the enemy was slowly but surely winning the battle.

Only one thing could save the island, and that was fighters. So, in April, the Americans joined the struggle, sending the USS *Wasp* to the Mediterranean with forty-seven more Spitfires. Within twenty-four hours, thirty of them had been wiped out, mostly on the ground, and the situation was as desperate as ever.

Now, in May, the *Wasp* and *Eagle* had joined forces in a do-or-die attempt to throw more fighters into the battle. The quietly-spoken Graham left his pilots with no illusions about the importance of the sixty-four Spitfires on the two carriers; they spelled the difference between life and death for the island, where a quarter of a million people were faced with the grim prospect of starvation. Sixty-four Spits might just be enough to turn the scales and win command of the air over Malta for long enough to enable vital supply convoys to break through to the island and unload their cargoes without being bombed to blazes. And Graham emphasized another grim possibility; if Malta fell, leaving the Axis supply lines unmolested, Rommel would very probably be in Cairo in the summer of 1942.

Graham's words had given Yeoman a lot to think about during the voyage southwards through the Atlantic. To think that he, together with sixty-three other young men from all over the British Commonwealth, and a few from the United States, could decide the fate of an entire people and possibly the outcome of the war in the Mediterranean, left him with an awesome weight of responsibility. He knew that once they reached Malta, they would fight as never before—and he knew that every single Spitfire had to get there.

It would be tough. Only one pilot, a man who had transferred to the RAF from the Fleet Air Arm, had ever taken off from an aircraft-carrier before, but there must be no errors, either on the take-off or the 600-mile flight to Malta that followed. Although every effort had been made to keep the operation a secret, Yeoman knew enough about the Germans' intelligence network to be certain that the enemy would know the Spitfires were coming. Anyway, they were bound to be picked up by radar at some point in their long flight. Navigation would have to be spot on, for if the Huns ran true to form the Messerschmitts would be lurking over the Sicilian coast, waiting to pounce on anybody who strayed off course. Also, the very length of the flight would stretch the

21

Spitfires to their limit, despite the addition of ninety-gallon auxiliary fuel tanks. Anyone who failed to achieve the best throttle setting and cruising speed for maximum range risked running out of juice a long way short of Malta.

Engine failure, too, was another nightmare possibility that lurked at the back of every pilot's mind. The single-engined fighter pilot who enjoyed flying over water for long distances hadn't been born, and if you had to ditch on this particular trip there would be no one around to fish you out. Still, they all had boundless confidence in the RAF engineering officer on board the *Wasp,* Squadron Leader Spence; he had fussed around the Spitfires constantly ever since they had left the Clyde, and his small team of fitters had nursed the Merlins lovingly. If anything failed, it would be no fault of theirs.

Flanked by her screen of destroyers, the *Wasp* had slipped through the Straits of Gibraltar under cover of darkness and made rendezvous with the rest of the naval force, consisting of HMS *Eagle*—whose Spitfires had arrived at Gibraltar in crates and been assembled there—the battleship HMS *Renown,* a cruiser and more destroyers.

Yeoman, as he went to his cabin to snatch a few hours' sleep on the evening of 8 May, had been almost sorry the voyage was nearly over. The Americans had been incredibly hospitable, the accommodation comfortable, and the food was excellent. At least, thought Yeoman, if we're heading for a starvation diet, we've been able to fill our bellies pretty well over the past few days.

Sleep had eluded him and he had gone up to the flight deck, through the small oval door at the base of the 'island', the carrier's superstructure. A stiff breeze was blowing and there was a heavy swell. He had ventured out some distance towards the middle of the deck, the wind whipping his clothing and refreshingly cool against his face. He had revelled in the mere task of keeping his balance on the great expanse of dipping, heaving metal. The night was moonless and the northern horizon was dark, but to the south, where the coastlines of Morocco and Algeria bordered the Mediterranean, the glittering lights of towns were clearly visible, and the sudden realization came upon him that the whole world was not at war. Yet the small section of which he formed a tiny part was, and as he strove to penetrate the darkness he could just make out the black outlines of the other ships, with the occasional phosphorescent flash of a bow wave. He was conscious, too, of eyes around him in the dark, as steel-helmeted lookouts peered at their designated sectors of sea, searching endlessly for the luminous track of a torpedo. The great ship never slept, and it was a comforting thought.

Now, seated in his Spitfire in the vibrating hangar deck, his impressions of the night before seemed unreal. Another glance at his watch: it was 5.25 a.m. An American air mechanic was making frantic signals to him and he snapped out of his reverie, reaching down to press the starter buttons. The big black propeller blades in front of him jerked spasmodically, then flickered and dissolved as the Merlin fired, adding its own voice to the giant roar. The needles of his instruments trembled, then crept slowly into their places, showing that all was well with temperatures and pressures in the heart of the Spitfire's nervous system. This was the world Yeoman knew, strapped inside the narrow confines of the metal cockpit, his own human nerves and senses linked through touch and sight and rubber umbilical cords to the finely tuned mechanics of his fighter, flesh and metal forged into a single entity whose task was to kill.

He was being pushed backwards on to the lift, a strange sensation, because he couldn't see behind him properly and he had a sudden panicky feeling that the Spit's tail was going to hit something. Then the mechanics disappeared, the lift gave a sudden lurch beneath him and the hangar deck began to recede.

A few moments later he emerged on the flight deck, blinking in the golden dawn. His wings were seized once more and the Spitfire trundled forward, leaving the lift free to descend. Two men in yellow overalls grabbed the fighter's tail, swinging it round so that the nose was pointing towards the bow. The carrier was forging ahead at twenty knots, and Yeoman could feel the wind buffeting the aircraft's fuselage.

He gave a quick glance round; overhead, a dozen Spitfires had just completed a circuit of the carrier and were setting course eastwards. That was Roger Graham's 'A' Flight; they would be well on their way by the time 'B' Flight, which Yeoman had been selected to lead, formed up.

Yeoman's eyes fastened on a man in a red skull-cap, balancing precariously on the deck a little to one side. His arms were raised in the air, his fists clenched. Yeoman put on the brakes. The man's hands began to describe rapid circles and Yeoman opened the throttle slowly. The engine roared and the Spitfire shuddered, straining against the brakes. She began to slide. Out of the corner of his eye Yeoman saw a checkered flag go down. He released the brakes and the Spitfire shot forward. He eased off the back pressure on the stick and the tail came up as the grey tower of the island flashed past.

The deck, which had seemed so huge last night, now looked ridiculously short. The bow dipped and Yeoman had a frightening glimpse of shimmering sea through the whirling propeller. Ruddering carefully to keep the aircraft straight, he pulled back the stick and the Spitfire bounced into the air as she reached flying speed, aided by the combined speed of the carrier's twenty knots and a thirty-knot headwind. The bow fell away below and behind and he pushed the stick forward ever so slightly, gently lowering the nose to gain a few extra knots. The flight deck was sixty feet above the sea, affording a nice little margin for this kind of manoeuvre. The speed built up comfortably and Yeoman pulled back the stick again, his other hand holding the throttle wide open, and brought the Spitfire up in a broad climbing turn, pulling up his flaps and undercarriage as he did so.

He circled the carrier, gaining height all the time, the warships looking like toys beneath his wings. One by one, the eleven other Spitfires of 'B' Flight took off and climbed to join him. Normally, twelve aircraft would have constituted a full squadron, but for the purposes of the flight to Malta the thirty-six Spitfires on the *Wasp* were split up into three separate formations, each one designated a Flight. Once on

24

the island, they would be shared out among the squadrons already there. 'A' and 'B' Flights, in other words the Spitfires led by Graham and Yeoman, were assigned to Luqa, while 'C' Flight, bringing up the rear, was to land at Takali.

With his Spitfires all in position, flying in three sections of four, Yeoman switched to his long-range tank and set course eastwards, into the glare of the rising sun. They climbed steadily to twenty thousand feet, flying due east. He looked to his left, and saw Gerry Powell's Spitfire riding smoothly on the warm currents of air, just where it should be. On Yeoman's right were the other two Spits of the leading section, flown by Sergeant Pilots McCallum and Wilcox, both of them Rhodesians. Completely inseparable on the ground, the two had spent the last few months flying fighter sweeps over France, and made a first-rate fighting team.

They had flown off the *Wasp* when she was almost directly abeam Algiers, and when Yeoman looked over to his right he could see clearly the ochre mountains of Algeria's coastal range. There was no sign of any other Spitfires, either in front or behind, but Yeoman knew that the carrier would by now have launched the twelve fighters of 'C' Flight and be turning back towards Gibraltar. HMS *Eagle*'s twenty-eight Spits were due to be launched half an hour later. The staggered times were to lessen the chances of the Spitfires all being caught on the ground by an enemy air strike. Each Spitfire was armed with two 20-mm cannon, which were loaded just in case, but the four .303 machine-guns had been removed to provide stowage in the wings for the pilots' kit. The aircraft were all Mks VC, with special tropical dust filters fitted under their noses.

The Spitfires droned steadily on, the burnished ball of the sun stabbing the pilots' eyeballs through their smoked glass goggles. As it climbed higher, a grey haze obscured the horizon and soon the mountains of Algeria were lost to sight. Yeoman maintained a steady heading, checking his compass and directional gyro frequently. The shadows of the cockpit made a welcome contrast to the glare outside; far below the sea was a sheet of blue-green glass.

They flew on for nearly three hours, the pilots stiff and cramped and soaked in sweat in their small, functional cockpits. Flying for long periods in a single-seat fighter was hell, for the dinghy packs on which the pilots sat felt as solid as concrete after a while, and no matter how one squirmed it was impossible to get comfortable.

Yeoman leaned forward suddenly in the cockpit, peering at a darker smudge that materialized slowly out of the haze, ahead and to the right. It grew more solid and became a spur of land, jutting out into the sea. He identified it quickly as Cape Bon, the northernmost tip of Tunisia, and smiled to himself, pleased with his navigation. They were right on track.

He waited until the cape was abeam his starboard wingtip, then turned gradually on to a south-easterly heading. The other Spitfires followed, as though tied to him by invisible threads. The next few minutes might be dangerous, because their new track took them close to the island of Pantellaria, where there were known to be German and Italian fighters. Yeoman would have liked to remind the pilots to keep their eyes peeled, but strict radio silence was in force all the way to Malta.

In the event, he need not have worried. The brown, rocky cone of Pantellaria slid by to starboard, and the Spitfires cruised on unmolested.

Yeoman looked at his watch; the time was 8.45. Malta should be coming up in another few minutes, and Yeoman sensed that all the pilots were straining their eyes for a sight of it. He understood their eagerness, for the fuel in the Spitfires' tanks was already getting too low for comfort.

The minutes ticked by. By 9.05 Yeoman was starting to become a little alarmed; they should have spotted Malta by now from this height, even in the haze. Well, he told himself, our navigation's been okay and they can't have moved the bloody place. It was bound to appear sooner or later.

He had hardly formed the thought when the haze far ahead of him seemed to change colour at one point. He blinked,

26

thinking at first that his eyes were playing tricks, but there was no mistaking the dark patch that rose from the sea—or rather two dark patches, the smaller one closest to the Spitfires. That would be Gozo, with Malta beyond it.

As the fighters drew nearer, the dark hue of the islands gave way to a russet colour; it was as though someone had tossed a couple of autumn leaves on the water. Gradually, as the Spitfires began their descent, more details emerged. Yeoman picked out steep cliffs, and beyond them a spider's web of white lines spreading across the parchment surface of Gozo, and he knew that they must be white stone walls. There were houses, too, sometimes in clusters, all of them white.

The radio burst into sudden life, startling Yeoman momentarily. The voice of the Malta fighter controller was rich and cultured.

'All Talbot aircraft, pancake. I repeat, all Talbot aircraft pancake. As fast as you can.'

Talbot was the call-sign of the reinforcement Spitfires. Malta's radar would have picked them up while they were still a long way out over the sea, and the controller, waiting until the last moment to avoid giving away their presence to the enemy, was telling them that it was safe to land—for the moment at least.

Down to four thousand feet now, and still descending, the Spitfires sped across Gozo and out over the blue channel that separated the two main islands. There was a third, tiny island in the channel, and Yeoman recalled that its name was Comino.

The whole of Malta was clearly visible now, its features leaping into sharp focus. In days, their names would be as familiar to Yeoman as his own, but now there was no time to register more than fleeting impressions. As they crossed the coast, Yeoman was puzzled at first by a strange, hazy pillar, like red smoke, that slanted up towards the sun, as though the core of the island was being dragged up to meet the sky. Then, with a sudden shock, he realized that he was looking at the dust kicked up by dozens of bomb bursts, drifting slowly on the breeze.

There was smoke, too, mingling with the dust, rising from an airfield that flashed beneath the Spitfires' wings. That must be Takali. Several objects, presumably aircraft, were burning on the ground. Away to the left, more smoke rose from the deep gash of Grand Harbour, with the tiers of white, flat-roofed houses, the multitude of baroque churches, yellow and soft against the sea, clustered all around it.

Luqa was dead ahead, its face ravaged by the smallpox of bomb craters. The Spitfires swept overhead, breaking into the circuit with wheels and flaps down. Glancing up, Yeoman spotted two or three more Spits higher up, covering them as they came in to land. The Spits circled, their shadows fleeting over the grey-green landscape, the white walls and stunted trees as they queued up on the approach to the only runway that still looked reasonably intact. Yeoman counted the aircraft of his flight as they landed ahead of him, one by one, bringing his own section in last of all. A quick glance above and behind, a roll of the head to make sure that there was nothing on his tail, and he slid back the cockpit canopy, throttling back and fishtailing to reduce speed. A couple of hundred yards ahead, Gerry Powell touched down in a cloud of dust and stones. Then it was Yeoman's turn. The Spitfire slid over some heaps of stone, the shattered wreck of an aircraft and a gravel track. Yeoman levelled out gently, easing back the stick and closing the throttle in one movement. The wheels touched, the Spitfire bounced slightly then settled down, rolling forward along the sun-baked strip.

Yeoman looked around him, not having any idea where to go next. Luqa was a scene of utter confusion, with Spitfires taxi-ing everywhere along bits of runway and winding tracks that disappeared into blast shelters and swarms of men in nondescript oddments of uniform running to and fro.

There was a sudden thump and Yeoman turned his head, startled. A lean, sunburned soldier was standing on the wing, clinging to the cockpit rail, grinning at him. The man bent forward and mouthed something, at the same time pointing with his free hand. Yeoman, his eardrums singing with the four-hour roar of the Merlin, was unable to make out what he was saying. The man pointed again, urgently, and Yeoman gathered that he wanted him to turn off the runway and follow one of the makeshift taxi-tracks. The pilot did as he was told, steering the Spitfire carefully round piles of stones which, he learned later, were distributed all around the airfield in readiness to fill in bomb craters.

At the end of the track a pen had been built, its walls constructed from sandbags and sand-filled petrol cans. He brought the Spitfire to a halt just short of it and, before he had time to make another move, he found himself practically lifted from the cockpit by a couple of burly airmen, one of whom switched off the fighter's engine. As Yeoman jumped stiffly down from the wing, already conscious of the intense heat, three more airmen seized the Spitfire by the tail and swung it round, dragging it backwards into the pen so that its nose was pointing out towards the airfield.

Yeoman was pushed unceremoniously aside while soldiers and airmen converged on the Spitfire from all sides, staggering under the weight of cans of fuel. Somebody removed the gun panels with a screwdriver and started throwing Yeoman's kit over his shoulder. The pilot, realizing that it was fruitless to protest and that there was a very good reason for all the haste, made a dive to pick it up out of the dust and got his fingers trodden on in the process. His kit was not all the Spitfire had borne across the Mediterranean in its wings; he watched in astonishment as an airman produced cartons of cigarettes, a box of what looked like medical supplies, assorted tools and a mosquito net from the other gun bays. Yeoman hadn't even known they were there, but it was clear that not an inch of room had been wasted.

Yeoman, completely ignored, stood in isolation on the fringe of all the turmoil and watched the airmen and soldiers breaking all records to refuel the Spitfire with the aid of a large funnel. There was no such luxury as a petrol bowser on Malta; everything had to be done laboriously by hand. Other airmen checked that the cannon were fully loaded—the

29

machine-guns would doubtless be fitted later—replaced the empty oxygen bottle with a full one and made sure the radio was in working order. In a couple of dozen more pens dotted round the airfield perimeter the same process was being re-enacted.

An ancient bus, its sides dented and riddled with holes, screeched to a stop outside the pen in a cloud of dust and a pilot jumped out, running towards Yeoman's Spitfire. Without a word to the newcomer he jumped up on the wing, reached into the cockpit, hurled Yeoman's parachute pack overboard and substituted his own.

'You didn't have to do that,' Yeoman protested. 'My chute is perfectly all right.'

'How the hell would I know?' the other answered curtly, in an accent that was either Australian or New Zealand. 'What I do know is that I packed mine myself, and it'll work all right. I'd get on the bus fast if I were you; there's a raid coming in.'

He swung himself into the cockpit and Yeoman turned away, clutching his parachute and his kit, most of which he had managed to retrieve. Someone was beckoning impatiently from the open door of the bus and he trotted across, recognizing Roger Graham. The bus was full of pilots, all of whom had flown in from the *Wasp*. Yeoman gathered that the vehicle had been dropping off pilots who were on readiness at each blast pen, and picking up the new arrivals.

He still had one leg out of the door when the driver lurched off with a crash of gears, and he would have fallen headlong into the dust if Graham had not reached out a hand to steady him. The vehicle careered off round the airfield perimeter, its occupants clinging on grimly as the driver swerved round craters and mounds of rubble. Through the glassless windows Yeoman caught sight of more blast pens, some empty, others filled with the charred remains of aircraft.

There was a shattering roar overhead and the pilots peered out of the windows, craning their necks to see what was going on. Spitfires were taking off in rapid succession, whipping up their wheels and flaps and climbing hard towards the north. Yeoman searched for the aircraft he had flown in from the carrier, but it was impossible to distinguish one from the other, for squadron code letters had been painted out.

The driver abruptly slammed on the brakes, throwing everyone in a heap on the floor, yelled 'G Shelter!' and vanished like lightning.

The pilots seized their belongings and tumbled out of the bus, blinking in the harsh sunlight and wondering what to do. There was nothing in their immediate vicinity except a long, low building surrounded by piles of shattered masonry. Somewhere, a siren began to wail.

A man wearing khaki battledress and tattered shorts appeared suddenly round one of the heaps of rubble, waving to them urgently. They ran across, panting under the weight of their gear, and as they turned the corner they found themselves in front of a narrow entrance, with a flight of steps leading down into the gloom.

They groped their way down the dark, twisting passage, which led through solid rock and was lit further on by solitary electric light bulbs, positioned at irregular intervals. As his eyes grew accustomed to the half-light Yeoman saw that alcoves had been carved out of the rock here and there along the passage to serve as makeshift offices or space for generators.

Eventually, they emerged into a large cavern, with benches around its walls and pin-up girls leering down incongruously from the tattered centre pages of magazines. Some of the benches were occupied by officers and airmen, who glanced uninterestedly at the newcomers before turning back to their newspapers. Yeoman and the others dropped thankfully into vacant spaces, grateful for the sudden coolness, looking about them in curiosity.

In the distance, the sirens were going full blast. Then there was a heavy silence followed by the thump of explosions. One or two of the new arrivals flinched and then glanced around them, clearly embarrassed and wondering if anyone had seen their momentary fear, but Yeoman could tell that the explosions were some way off.

To no one in particular, the man in the battledress, who Yeoman now saw wore a squadron leader's braid on his epaulettes, announced:

'They're going for Takali. Thought so. We had the bastards at eight o'clock. I'm going up to watch the fun. Anyone coming?'

He disappeared back up the steps, followed by Yeoman, Roger Graham and one or two of the others. From their vantage-point outside the entrance to the shelter they had an excellent view across the valley that sloped away to the north of Luqa, towards Takali. Aircraft, looking like black crows in the distance, were wheeling and diving through a spatter of anti-aircraft bursts. Black smoke boiled up from the ground, towering over the stricken airfield.

The enemy aircraft sped away, pursued by a handful of darting fighters. Yeoman glanced at his watch: the attack had lasted barely five minutes, but it had been timed to perfection. Yeoman realized that much of the smoke he could see must be rising from HMS *Eagle*'s newly-landed Spitfires, burning on the ground.

A distant siren moaned the all-clear. It was picked up by others, until the whole island seemed to ring with the sound.

'Well, that's knackered that, good and proper,' the Squadron Leader said in disgust. 'Come on, let's go and have a drink.'

He led the way to a small stone hut that served as the officers' mess. There was just one room, with a square of threadbare carpet on the floor and a makeshift bar across one corner. The others emerged from the shelter in ones and twos and joined them. Someone produced a crate of Farson's, the local brew; it was lukewarm, but the pilots, parched after their long flight across the sea, gulped it down blissfully.

After a while, some of the pilots who had taken off to intercept the enemy raid began to trickle in. They looked hollow-eyed and exhausted, and Yeoman sensed that they had no desire to talk. He searched the face of each man who came in, trying to recognize the pilot who had taken his own Spitfire into action, but there was no sign of him.

They found his body two days later, dashed to pieces among some rocks on Gozo. The grisly discovery was made by a goatherd, attracted to the spot by a streamer of white silk that fluttered from the dead man's parachute pack.

The rest of the canopy had failed to open.

Chapter Three

Although it was early evening the day had lost little of its heat, and the pilots, crammed together on the seats of the ramshackle bus, were thankful for the steady flow of air that streamed through the vehicle's shattered windscreen. Yeoman, lost in thought, stared through a side window at the vast contrast of colours that whirled past: the yellowish-white of stone walls, the pink of churches on the skyline, the grey-green of the land itself, dappled now with shadow.

The sky, a vault of rich blue stretching endlessly above them, was empty for once. It had been a confused, bewildering day, with several air raids, and Yeoman had spent most of it in G Shelter, together with the other reinforcement pilots. Any hope they had entertained of getting into action quickly had been rudely dashed; the veteran pilots of the squadron on Luqa had been eagerly awaiting the arrival of the new Spitfires for a long time, and they had no intention of letting the newcomers fly them. Yeoman knew that this was a matter of wisdom, rather than of selfishness; he had already learned that Malta was a far different battleground from any he and his fellow pilots had experienced so far, with different —almost alien—rules and tactics, and unless the newcomers were initiated gradually they wouldn't last five minutes.

The proof of that was starkly evident in the day's losses. Yeoman reckoned that one-third, perhaps more, of the Spitfires which had flown in from the two carriers had already been put out of action, either in the air or on the ground.

Another couple of days at this pace, and Malta's air defences would be back to square one.

The bus churned its way up a steep hill. Craning his neck to see over the heads of the pilots seated on his right, Yeoman picked out a flat expanse of ground, a hillside broken by the dark, yawning mouths of caves, and some sandbagged emplacements. He glimpsed the tail of a Spitfire and knew that they were passing Takali. Although the airfield had been bombed three times that day there was no sign of damage, nor indeed of any movement whatsoever.

The bus churned its way up the hill, twisting round bends, and suddenly the shadows of high walls fell across it. The driver threaded his way deftly through narrow streets, some of them showing signs of severe bomb damage, and through occasional openings Yeoman caught tantalizing glimpses of ancient, curved archways and baroque churches. He leaned forward and tapped the shoulder of Roger Graham, who was sitting in front of him, and asked where they were.

'Rabat,' the squadron leader replied. 'It's the old capital of Malta. It used to be called Melita—that's where the island gets its name from—and, according to legend, Saint Paul stayed here after he was shipwrecked.'

The road narrowed even further and the bus passed slowly through an archway, a gate into some inner sanctum enclosed by vast stone walls.

'We're in M'dina now,' Graham continued. 'These walls were built by the Arabs to fortify Melita when they occupied the place after the Romans had gone, and the bit left outside they called rabat; the name means simply "suburb". When the Spaniards occupied the island they changed its name to Città Notabile. Then the Knights came along and made Malta their HQ, so to speak; they built Valletta, which is really one big fortress, and moved the capital there. After that M'dina took second place, but to many Maltese it's still the capital; they call it the Città Vecchia, or Old City.'

Yeoman was about to question Graham further when the bus halted outside a palace, its walls golden in the rays of the sinking sun to a point just above a massive iron-bound double door, where the shadows of neighbouring buildings cast dark, angular lines across them.

'Right,' Graham shouted, 'everybody out. This is it.'

They piled out of the bus and into the palace, their shoes kicking up small clouds of the grey dust that lay like a mantle over everything as they went. Just before he reached the massive door, Yeoman noticed another khaki-painted bus parked up a side street, and guessed that it had brought more pilots over from Takali. All the new arrivals were to be briefed here at the same time.

As they went inside Yeoman shivered slightly. The gloom of the big hall was dank and forbidding, in sharp contrast to the sunlight outside. Once, he thought, the whole place must have been filled with light and laughter; now its walls held only the musty odour of dead dynasties. The pilots crossed the hall quickly, their footsteps echoing, and climbed a wide marble staircase. At its head was a long corridor, and at the end of the corridor a wooden door stood open, giving access to a large room. A hubbub of voices, punctuated by an occasional laugh, drifted from it.

The room was crowded with pilots, perched astride chairs and benches, on trestle tables and window ledges. A few nodded and smiled at the Luqa contingent as they trooped in, pushing their way into the throng in search of vacant places. Yeoman looked around him, trying to pick out any familiar faces, but failed to locate any. He sat down on a bench between Roger Graham and Gerry Powell and waited to see what was going to happen.

The wait was a brief one. After only a couple of minutes, a voice from the doorway cut through the buzz of chatter like a knife.

'Gentlemen!'

Chairs and benches clattered as they stood up, staring fixedly ahead of them. A man came into Yeoman's field of vision, striding purposefully down the centre of the room towards the heavy table at its far end. He went round it, laid his cap carefully on the table top, and stood with his hands behind his back, surveying the men assembled in front of him. A thick-set, medium-built man, he seemed to radiate strength. Although his grey hair betrayed the fact that he was more than twice the age of most of the pilots in the room, his eyes were sharp and piercing, his manner full of vigour. He wore full khaki-drill uniform, immaculately pressed. The cap on the trestle table beside him bore a double row of gold oak leaves around its peak.

This was the man who, in May 1942, bore the burden of what was probably the most difficult command in the Royal Air Force: the Air Officer Commanding Malta, Air Vice-Marshal Hugh P. Lloyd.

'Sit down, gentlemen.'

The chairs scraped and clattered again and a ripple of coughs ran round the room before silence returned. The Air Vice-Marshal spoke.

'Welcome to Malta, gentlemen. I'm sorry the Luftwaffe decided to welcome you first.' The remark brought a murmur of laughter.

'I am not going to make a lengthy speech,' the AVM continued, 'but I do want to impress one or two points upon you. Firstly, I fought the Germans in the last war, and now I am fighting them again in this. Why? Because they are bullies. They want to bully Malta into submission, but they won't succeed, because we are going to stop them.'

The AVM smiled briefly. 'In this determination I am totally at one with the new Governor-General of Malta. Some of you may have heard of him. He is Field-Marshal Lord Gort.'

Yeoman's ears pricked up and he listened to the AVM's words with renewed interest. In a flash, his memory reeled off details of the man who had arrived on Malta in the hour of her desperate need. John Standish Surtees Prendergast Vereker, sixth Viscount Gort; the man who had become almost a legend during his service with the Grenadier Guards in the Great War. Wounded four times, mentioned in dispatches nine times for galantry, he had won the Military Cross, the Distinguished Service Order three times over, and finally the Victoria Cross.

In May 1940, when Yeoman had flown Hurricanes in

France, Gort had been commander of the British Expeditionary Force, and later had been unjustly blamed for authorizing the BEF's retreat to Dunkirk. Yeoman knew otherwise; if Gort's men had not begun their fighting retreat across Flanders when they did, with Allied armies collapsing all around, they would have been encircled by the Germans and the 'deliverance of Dunkirk' would never have happened. As far as Yeoman was concerned, the choice of this man as Malta's Governor-General was inspired. If anyone could sustain the island's morale through the onslaught, and God only knew how long it would last, then that someone was the unassuming bulldog figure of 'Tiger' Gort.

'We are aware,' the Air Vice-Marshal went on, 'that the Germans and Italians are planning to invade Malta. We do not know when. But we do know this: that they will never invade until they have established complete air superiority.'

He paused, then, pointing a finger to lend emphasis to his words, told them briskly:

'You are here to deny them that superiority. You, together with the anti-aircraft defences, are Malta's shield. The Maltese people are taking everything the enemy throws at them, and will continue to endure as long as they see you in the air, day after day, fighting to preserve their homes and ideals.'

The AVM paused again, letting his words sink in, and then continued:

'For the present, Malta is on the defensive. But never forget that the island's true strategic role is an offensive one. From here, our bombers and torpedo aircraft can strike hard at the enemy's supply lines in the Mediterranean, but they cannot do so without your protection. Your task, therefore, is to secure the skies over Malta to a degree that will render an enemy invasion out of the question, and to enable our bomber and torpedo squadrons to return and get on with the business of hammering the enemy.'

Not a man stirred. They were all gripped by the plain, unvarnished facts presented to them by the AVM. Yeoman was reminded irrationally of a father, telling his sons the facts of life. The AVM's eyes roved round the room, seeking out the face of each man and holding it briefly, as though the message in his words was addressed to him personally and to no other.

'There is, however, a more immediate task. You men who arrived this morning have brought only a temporary respite. Let us be under no illusion; Malta is starved of every conceivable commodity, from food to fuel. People will not function without one, Spitfires and Hurricanes without the other. More convoys must reach the island if we are to survive, and once here they must be permitted to unload without interference from the enemy. There must be no repetition of the events of previous weeks, when several ships, having braved everything to bring their vital cargoes to Malta, were sunk in Grand Harbour before they could unload.'

The AVM folded his arms and stared at them.

'Fighters would have prevented that disaster,' he went on, 'but we had too few. It must not, will not, happen again. You, gentlemen, are Malta's salvation. The next convoy to reach Malta will deliver its supplies, and will do so because of your efforts.

'Let me conclude by saying this. Here and now, you may hate every moment of your time on Malta. But looking back, in years to come, you will realize that you have been part of a first rate team, and be proud of that fact. Good luck to you all.'

The pilots rose again as the AVM left the room. There was no time to dwell on his words, because his place was taken immediately by a tall, swarthy officer whose face seemed to show the signs of a recent illness. He introduced himself to the men.

'My name is Hazell, and I am Wing Commander (Flying) at Takali. I have been asked to give you a few pointers to the way we live and operate out here. You will, of course, be briefed more fully within your own units tomorrow.' He cleared his throat and looked around, as though in search of a glass of water. Finding none, he coughed again and continued:

'First of all, I know that some of you have gained a considerable degree of experience elsewhere. Now, I'm not going to ask you to forget all you have learned; that would be foolish. I want you to remember, however, that we follow a completely different set of rules out here, and some of you may find them bewildering. For a start we are always heavily outnumbered, and therefore we have to improvise all the time. No sortie ever follows the same pattern as the next —nothing like the big fighter sweeps some of you will have taken part in.

'We are here to shoot down bombers. Remember that always. The fighters we leave alone whenever possible; we don't tangle with them unless it's absolutely unavoidable, and then only at the last moment. Things tend to happen very quickly, too, and there is often no time for the niceties of R/T procedure such as you have been used to. We use first names a lot. Things such as "Yellow Two, break starboard" are all very well, but by the time you've got it out Yellow Two will probably be going down in flames. Something like "Break, Fred" serves just as well, and you save a vital second.

'Similarly, enemy fighters are always "snappers", no matter what they are. Don't waste time trying to identify something as a One-oh-Nine, or a Macchi or a Reggiane; if it looks unfriendly it's a snapper, and you make sure everybody knows it's there.'

The wing commander paused in mid-stride, waved a hand and said, 'Oh, by the way, sorry, chaps—smoke if you want to.' He produced a cigarette case, extracted a cigarette and lit it. A look of bliss spread over his face. 'Ah, Camels,' he said, 'Thank God for a decent smoke. We've had nothing but bloody Drapis, that's the local brand, for weeks now. They make 'em out of goat shit.'

He inhaled deeply, then went on with his briefing.

'Talking about fighters,' he said, 'you've probably heard a lot of bloody nonsense about the Italians. Forget it. Our experience here has shown that the Eyeties will stay and fight

40

like hell while the Germans are high-tailing it for home. Anybody met the Italians before?'

Yeoman stuck up his hand self-consciously. 'Just once,' he said, 'over Libya. It was a Fiat G.50, and it gave me a few nasty moments.' Once again, he was uncomfortably aware that his thirteen victories made him an old boy among the new boys, in a manner of speaking.

'Well,' said Hazell, 'the ones we meet over here are Macchi 200s and 202s, and Reggiane 2000s. They are all highly manoeuvrable, the latter perhaps more than the other two, so watch out for them. As far as the Huns are concerned, they are all pretty much textbook fighters, hanging around upstairs and making fast firing passes before climbing back up again. You really have to keep your eyes peeled, because they can be on top of you before you know what's happening, especially if there's haze about.

'In one respect,' Hazell went on, 'we are very fortunate indeed. We have a first-rate fighter controller, Group Captain Douglas. He was a sector controller in the Battle of Britain, and came here straight from handling the big fighter sweeps over France. He really is a bloody good type, so do what he tells you. He was to have been here in person to have a word with you, but he's tied up at a conference in Valletta.

'We always operate in pairs here; it's very rarely that we are able to put up more than four fighters in one place. With all the opposition we have to contend with it's very easy to become separated, and if that happens in the middle of a scrap make a beeline for the nearest airfield and no messing about. If you're chased by fighters, head for Takali and do tight turns inside the defensive ring of Bofors guns.'

Yeoman glanced round. Some of the pilots were scribbling notes on bits of paper or the back of cigarette packets as Hazell talked. He went on for a few more minutes, describing tactics and answering the occasional question that was fired at him. Finally, he glanced at his watch, placed both hands on the table and leaned forward, staring intently at the pilots.

'There's one last thing,' he said. 'This is not a game of cricket. We are fighting a dirty, nasty war out here, and those

41

bastards over there are pulling no punches. There have been instances of our chaps being machine-gunned after they baled out. Now I'm not suggesting you do the same, but if you do, nobody is going to take much notice. Personally, I shoot the bastards. Just think about it, that's all.'

'Well,' said Yeoman to Roger Graham a few minutes later, as they boarded the bus once more. 'I've never heard anyone put it as bluntly as that before. Still, I don't think I would be prepared to shoot a defenceless pilot, especially one who is likely to be taken prisoner anyway.'

Graham looked at him. 'Larry Hazell has his reasons,' he said quietly. 'I've known him a long time. He was a Spit pilot with the Biggin Hill wing in the Battle of Britain, then his wife and three kids were killed during the night raids on Liverpool, and after that he transferred to night-fighters. He shot ten Huns down, then the action slowed down a bit so he came out here. The last I heard, he had twenty-two kills to his credit. He's a little bit round the bend, the way he goes after those bombers. He just ignores return fire completely, and gets stuck in. It's a miracle he's still in one piece.'

The bus followed the narrow road north-eastwards from M'dina, winding its way through the streets of Mosta, the ancient city that was dominated by the second largest domed cathedral in Europe. It was growing darker now, and the buildings on either side were little more than looming shadows, all the more fascinating because of their obscurity. Yeoman sat and smoked his pipe, conscious of the dark shapes of his fellow pilots around him, swaying to the movement of the vehicle. He was tired now, and grimy with the dust of Malta. Idly he wondered if it was going to be possible to have a bath; he doubted it, if the water situation was as bad as he had been led to believe.

Billets for the Luqa pilots had been found in the hilltop town of Naxxar, a mile or so beyond Mosta. They were quartered in what seemed to be yet another old palace; it was by no means as large as the one in M'dina, but was spacious enough. By the light of flickering candles they groped their way up a stone staircase and out on to a broad landing. There

42

were rooms on either side, most of them filled with sleeping bodies sprawled on mattresses, but Graham led the way along a series of corridors to another landing, where smaller cubicles stood vacant. Three pilots were allocated to each room, Yeoman sharing his with Gerry Powell and another flight lieutenant, Arthur Rowland. The whole building stank of stale cooking, human sweat and drains. Maltese orderlies brought round pannikins of bully stew and mugs of tea, and after eating their first real meal that day the pilots turned in and tried to get some sleep.

It proved impossible, for the newcomers at least. The raiders came that night, and Malta trembled to the constant crash of explosions and the bark of anti-aircraft guns. Flashes of light burst eerily across the interior of the room. Fine dust trickled down from the ceiling, tickling throats and nostrils.

By midnight Yeoman could stand it no longer. He got up, pulled on his trousers and groped his way out on to the balcony, tripping over Rowland en route and ignoring the latter's 'Lie down, for God's sake, you silly sod!'

The balcony faced south-east, towards Valletta. There was a moon, and from Yeoman's relatively high vantage-point the ragged outline of Grand Harbour, with its surrounding clusters of buildings, was clearly visible. The flashes of bombs and guns threw the distant shapes of twin-spired churches into sharp relief. Shell-bursts spewed across the sky, following the direction of probing searchlight beams. Yeoman calculated that Naxxar was a good five miles from Valletta, but even at this distance the noise was terrific, the thunderous drumroll of explosions blotting out the sound of the bombers' engines.

Suddenly, something caught Yeoman's eye and he turned his head, peering into the darkness behind St. Julian's Bay. High over the sea, a stream of sparks danced in the night. A few moments later, cutting through the rumble from Valletta, the high-pitched bark of quick-firing cannon reached him.

He smiled, exulting quietly. One of Malta's small force of twin-engined Bristol Beaufighter night-fighters must be on the prowl. The sparks flashed again, and this time a pinpoint of white light flickered at the spot where they converged. As Yeoman watched it grew in intensity, like an exploding star. Then it began to fall, slowly at first and then faster. It flared brightly and split into a dozen fragments. They fell like meteors, each one trailing its own small tail of fire, to be abruptly extinguished in the blackness of the Mediterranean. There would be empty spaces at the breakfast table in some German or Italian mess this morning.

Yeoman continued to watch, scanning the sky, but he saw no further combats. After a while the anti-aircraft barrage from Valletta died away and the searchlights flicked out one by one. The receding throb of engines reached him now as the raiders droned away northwards towards Sicily.

An aircraft flew overhead, very low, its dark shape fleeting briefly across the stars, its engines strangely muted. One of the Beaufighters was returning to Takali. Idly, he wondered if it was the one whose gunfire he had watched a few minutes earlier.

He thought suddenly of the enemy aircrew whose lives he had just seen extinguished. The light breeze that blew off the sea was chilly, but that was not the reason a shiver ran through him. He turned and went indoors, wondering what the morning would bring.

Chapter Four

Yeoman sat on the sandbags that formed the walls of the blast pen, feeling desperately tired. It seemed as though he had been asleep for only a few minutes before Roger Graham, candle in hand, had shaken him awake. There had been one consolation; the water supply was working, so he had been able to avail himself of a quick cold bath and a shave before leaving for Luqa, together with a dozen other red-eyed pilots.

It had still been dark when they arrived at the airfield, and Graham had delivered a rapid briefing under the flickering lights of G Shelter. Yeoman had learned then why the enemy had paid so much attention to Valletta during the night. Under cover of darkness a fast minelayer had docked in Grand Harbour, carrying a load of vital anti-aircraft ammunition. Without it, Malta's guns would have fallen silent within forty-eight hours.

With the dawn, teams of soldiers, sailors and Maltese workers were still striving to unload the vessel. The enemy had failed to destroy her during the night, so it was certain that the bombers would come again in daylight. At all costs the RAF had to stop them, to break up their formations before they reached Grand Harbour. Every serviceable fighter would be in the air when the alarm went up: that amounted to a dozen Spitfires from Luqa, ten more from Takali and four Hurricanes from Hal Far. It was hoped that several more fighters, damaged during the air attacks of the previous day, would be ready by mid-morning.

Yeoman had spent the first couple of hours of daylight getting to know his fitter and rigger, Sykes and Tozer, both of them leading aircraftmen. Sykes was in a bad way, and kept reeling round the end of the blast pen to be sick. He had fallen victim to the 'Malta Dog', a particularly nasty kind of amoebic dysentery caused by eating the island's vegetables, which were nurtured in highly fertilized soil. Everyone, Sykes told Yeoman grimly between spasms, got the Dog sooner or later; it usually lasted only a couple of days, but it shattered a man completely. Pilots who contracted the disease were grounded immediately, but ground crews usually worked on and made the best of it.

This morning's operations were strictly for experienced pilots only. Those among the newcomers with no combat experience would have to kick their heels on the ground, receiving their baptism of fire in days to come when things were perhaps a little quieter. Even Yeoman, who was far from being a novice, was to fly as Roger Graham's number two. He could see Graham now, seated like himself on the sandbags of another blast pen seventy yards away. He waved, but the squadron leader was engrossed in a book and appeared not to notice.

'Look, sir,' Tozer said suddenly, 'why not come down here and have a bit of a rest?' He indicated a small tent the two airmen had rigged up as defence against both the heavy early morning dew and the intense heat of the day. 'This sun's going to get bloody hot before long.'

Yeoman looked at his watch. It was already nearly nine o'clock, and amazingly the enemy bombers had not yet put in an appearance.

'No, thanks,' he said, smiling. 'If I lie down in there I'll never get up again.'

He slid down from the sandbags and wandered over to the Spitfire, leaning against one of the cannons. The metal was already warm to the touch. The uncanny silence, after the noise of the previous night, was beginning to get on his nerves. He felt slightly dizzy, and there was an uncomfortable churning sensation in the pit of his stomach.

He looked at Tozer. 'How long have you been out here?' he asked.

Tozer shrugged 'About thirteen months, sir,' he answered. 'Now old Sykes here'—he waved a hand towards his pale and shaking colleague—'has been here nearly two years.' He grinned. 'You'd think he'd be used to it by now, wouldn't you, sir?'

Yeoman made no reply. Two years of this hell, he thought. Sykes must have experienced it all, from the very first Italian air raids. He looked at the man with profound admiration.

Sykes coughed and said weakly, 'It wasn't bad at first, sir, when we just had the Italians to contend with. Many of the Eyeties didn't seem too interested in attacking us at all. I once saw three bombers circle well off the coast, drop their bombs in the sea and head for home. Other blokes have seen the same thing happen. Then Jerry arrived, and it was a different story.' He spat into the dust. 'They're bastards, they are.'

'Yes, sir,' Tozer said, 'old Sykes was here during the first big blitz, January to March '41. I got here in April, when things had died down a bit. Jerry was invading Greece and Crete then, and had pulled most of his bombers out of Sicily. They came back in the autumn, though, and we've had it just about non-stop ever since. Still,' he grinned, 'can't let the bastards grind us down, can we, sir?'

Yeoman shook his head. The unfailing cheerfulness and adaptability of the RAF's ground crews never ceased to amaze him. These men on Malta lived a troglodyte's existence in a series of caves cut into the walls of old quarries, stifling burrows thick with the stench of old sump oil that was used for cooking; the caves were roasting by day and freezing by night, and yet their morale was as high as any he had seen anywhere. Higher, perhaps, for on Malta everyone was pretty much in the same boat, and as a result everyone felt himself to be part of a closely-knit team.

Yeoman looked up at the northern sky and drummed his fingertips impatiently on the metal surface of his Spitfire's wing. Where the hell were the Huns? This waiting was beginning to get him down. There had already been four false alarms that morning, and after each one the knot in his stomach had got that little bit tighter. He supposed he ought to have been sitting in the cockpit, ready to go, but the heat in that confined space was murderous. As it was, his shirt was already soaked in sweat under his Mae West lifejacket. The rest of his clothing consisted of shorts, socks and desert boots; although it would be bitterly cold at heights of over twenty thousand feet, to wear heavier clothing on the ground was to risk heat-stroke.

Suddenly, his heart leapt into his mouth. In Luqa village, the sirens had begun to wail. Another false alarm? He peered towards G Shelter through the heat haze that danced and shimmered over the airfield.

Two red lights arc'd up into the hot air, followed by two more an instant later. Scramble!

Yeoman grabbed his helmet from the Spitfire's wing, pulling it on as he stepped into the cockpit and settled down on his parachute pack. He strapped himself in quickly, with a semi-automatic reflex born of long practice.

The Merlin—God bless Rolls-Royce!—choked a couple of times, then started with a bang. Long flames shot briefly from the exhausts. Yeoman reached up and slammed the hood closed. Furnace-like though the cockpit was, to taxi with the hood open was to risk being half choked to death by clouds of swirling dust. One of the airmen, Tozer, had jumped up on the wingroot and was hanging on with one hand, battered by the wind from the propeller, grinning and waving. Yeoman realized that he was wishing him good luck and gave him a thumbs-up; Tozer dropped out of sight.

Yeoman released the brakes, opened the throttle a little and took the Spitfire out of the blast pen on to the rough track that converged on the runway. Over to the left Roger Graham's fighter was also moving forward, dragging the inevitable dust-cloud in its wake. More dust, billowing up from various points around the field, betrayed the whereabouts of other taxiing Spitfires.

He swung into position behind and to the right of Graham, swinging the Spitfire's long nose from side to side to ensure that there were no obstacles in his path. Graham's Spitfire was a grey ghost in its shroud of dust. They turned on to the runway, opening their throttles. Yeoman, from force of habit, gave a quick glance over his shoulder. This was the dangerous time, the time when Messerschmitts might come streaking down, shark-like, to strafe and destroy.

The sky behind was clear. Out of the corner of his eye Yeoman spotted another pair of Spits, their tails already up, roaring down Luqa's secondary runway. That must be the other two aircraft in Graham's section, flown by Gerry Powell and one of the Rhodesian sergeants, McCallum. They were wasting no time, and Yeoman realized that he and Graham would cross the runway intersection only a couple of seconds before the other two fighters.

Ahead of him, Graham's fighter lifted into the air, shedding its cloud of dust. Yeoman's Spitfire, its tail now up, hit a patch of uneven surface and lurched violently. He worked the rudder pedals frantically, striving to keep the aircraft straight, and eased back the stick. The fighter bounced once, then left the uneven surface of the runway. Yeoman kept the nose down for a few seconds, building up speed, then pulled up sharply after Graham, who was turning steeply to the right on a northerly heading.

As they climbed, Graham's voice burst over the R/T, calling up Group Captain Douglas at the operations room in Valletta.

'Hello, Douggie, this is Catfish Leader. Any gen?'

The reply came back immediately, in Douglas's rich, reassuring tones.

'Catfish Leader, Roger, thirty plus big jobs and twenty plus little jobs approaching Gozo, Angels fifteen to twenty. Grab Angels quickly.'

Douglas was telling them that thirty bombers, escorted by at least twenty fighters, were on their way to Malta, stacked up between fifteen and twenty thousand feet. Furthermore, he was ordering them to gain altitude as quickly as possible.

Yeoman, taking his eyes away from Graham's Spitfire for an instant, glanced over to his left, towards Grand Harbour. The three deep inlets were crowned by a layer of bronze haze, and beneath it, spreading like some foul poison, was a carpet of some strange grey-green substance. Yeoman was reminded for a moment of his father's stories of gas, creeping over the trenches in the Great War, then he realized that he was looking at a smoke-screen, put up by the harbour defences to conceal the all-important minelayer.

The Spitfires swept on, climbing all the time, over the pock-marked lunar surface of Takali. Looking down, Yeoman saw long dust-trails as fighters took off; the Spitfires themselves were invisible in the haze.

Roger Graham's fighter was two hundred yards ahead and well over to the left. Yeoman turned his head, watching as the other two Spits of the section jockeyed into position half a mile away. This was the classic Malta formation: four fighters, widely spaced, each pilot covering his neighbour.

Malta was falling away behind them now, a grey blur beneath the curtain of haze. The sea was brassy ahead of them, with the ragged outline of Comino Island and Gozo beyond it.

'Catfish Leader, this is Douggie. Vector-oh-one-oh.'

The four Spitfires turned gently to the right, on to the new heading the controller had passed to them. Below and behind them, still lost in the haze, Yeoman sensed more fighters climbing hard, and the knowledge that they were not alone was reassuring.

Automatically, Yeoman checked his instruments as they speared upwards, keeping a constant eye on engine temperatures and pressures. He lowered his seat, which had been raised for take-off to give maximum visibility, so that it was below the level of the armour plating behind him. He found that he was trembling slightly, and willed himself to relax.

The Spitfires burst out of the haze at eight thousand feet and went on climbing. Yeoman turned his oxygen fully on and looked around. The sky and sea merged into a single cerulean backdrop; it was like flying inside a luminous blue ball and the light was painful to the eyes, even through tinted goggles. Far below, and dropping steadily behind, Malta resembled a splotch of dried cow manure, staining the purity of the sea.

Fourteen thousand feet, and still no sign of the enemy. Graham began to weave gently from side to side and Yeoman followed him, searching the sky endlessly. Suddenly, ahead of them, four white puffs of smoke appeared like golf balls high over Gozo. They were pointers; the anti-aircraft gunners were showing the fighters the way.

'Catfish Leader, Zebra plus eight. Acknowledge.'

'Roger, Douggie, Zebra plus eight. Got the pointers.'

From his operations room in Valletta, Group Captain Douglas was telling them that the enemy bombers and fighters were over Gozo at twenty-six thousand feet. The Spitfires hurtled on, climbing hard, throttles wide open, striving to get above the still invisible enemy.

More flak-bursts blossomed out, below and to the left. Then still more, higher this time, almost level with the Spitfires. Yeoman swore inwardly; the sky seemed empty. The ack-ack must be firing at 109s; the bastards were so small that it was often impossible to pick them out in the glare until they were right on top of you.

A black shadow fleeted over Yeoman's cockpit and he looked up, startled, but it was only the other two Spitfires in the section, crossing over himself and Graham, covering them.

Search, he told himself. Search the sky, and live. Keep your eyes skinned. The turns were made so that the sun was always behind them, and he suddenly knew what Graham was up to; if there were Messerschmitts lurking up there, he was trying to tempt them down, to 'suck them in' as the pilots said in their jargon, and keep them occupied while the Takali and Hal Far fighters went for the bombers, wherever they were.

The roar of the engine became part of his senses. He was enclosed in a strange, unreal silence. Watch it, his brain screamed, don't drift, keep your mind on the job. Twenty-five thousand feet. Christ, but it was cold. A thin stream of air was entering the cockpit from somewhere, freezing his bare arms.

Where the hell were they? Searching, searching above, across and behind, forcing his eyeballs to relax. Don't strain, you see nothing that way. The sun was a great white ball of icy light that seared the eyes but did not warm the flesh.

Catfish Red Three was calling, his voice garbled and distorted. Yeoman could make out only Gerry Powell's call-sign. The garbled words took on a higher pitch, then suddenly burst over the radio with stark clarity.

'Snappers, four o'clock high!'

Yeoman craned his neck, fighting the constriction of his seat harness to peer over his right shoulder. He could see nothing. Where, for Jesus' sake, where were they?

Then he saw them, a shoal of dark crosses, curving round behind the Spitfires from the right, coming round to seven o'clock and turning in. The Spits were level now, holding a steady course with the sun behind and slightly to the left.

The Messerschmitts were shadowing them, keeping pace. Graham turned again, as though intent on searching the sky below. Over the R/T Group Captain Douglas's voice came again, momentarily distracting, warning them of more fighters climbing over Filfla, the small island three miles to the south-west of Malta. The bastards must have come in low under the radar, thought Yeoman. Never mind, they were still some distance away. The immediate concern was for the Messerschmitts above and behind.

'Look out, here they come. Wait for it.'

Roger Graham's voice was calm and unruffled. The Spitfires went on turning and the Messerschmitts turned with them, levelling out and arrowing in from astern, using the speed they had built up in their dive to overhaul the British fighters. Yeoman counted ten of them: not too long odds, for Malta.

Yeoman's hands were sweaty and slippery on the stick. The leading 109s were growing larger in one corner of his rear-view mirror. God, would Graham never order them to break? The enemy fighters were close, far too close! If the break didn't come in another second he was going to do it anyway, and to hell with the consequences. . . .

'Break left!'

They stood their Spitfires on their wingtips, hauling sticks back into their stomachs. The four fighters came round in a turn that crushed the pilots down in their seats, dragged down the flesh of their cheeks. Yeoman's mouth sagged open with the brute force of it and he felt suddenly sick. Three 109s flashed overhead, their tracers punching holes in thin air, and Graham reversed his turn, following them. Yeoman clung to the squadron leader's gyrating Spitfire in desperation and saw Graham open fire, still in the turn, his cannon shells finding their mark in a 109 which suddenly belched white smoke, toppled over and went down vertically. Then Graham reversed his turn yet again, facing the other Messerschmitts, and once more a great fist rammed Yeoman's body down, punching the air from his struggling lungs.

A 109 shot across his nose and he fired, hopelessly, for the deflection angle was impossible, and almost cried out aloud in amazement when the enemy fighter's tail disintegrated. The 109 flicked away below and he saw no more of it; he would only be able to claim a 'damaged'.

He glanced around, and miraculously the 109s had gone, for the moment at least. All four Spitfires were still with one another, joining up into their section formation as Graham curved out of his turn into level flight.

Yeoman had the oddest sensation of no longer being master of his own fate. All he knew was that he had to cling to Roger Graham's Spitfire like a leech, alternately watching its manoeuvres and tearing his eyes away from it to search the sky, hoping to God that Powell and McCallum were doing their job and guarding the section's blind spots.

'Snappers five o'clock, high!'

'Snappers three o'clock, level!'

Oh Christ, they were coming in from all sides. Which way to turn? Which way? Then, once again, Graham's calm voice, restoring a measure of sanity, its very tones encouraging them to relax and keep their wits about them.

'Wait for it, chaps. The high jobs are ours. Wait for the break!'

He was coolly telling them to ignore the Messerschmitts boring in from three o'clock, and to concentrate on the ones astern. Then Yeoman suddenly knew why. Climbing hard under the Messerschmitts over on the right were half a dozen more Spitfires, coming from God knew where. Yeoman hadn't noticed them until this moment, and it didn't look as though the Germans had spotted them at all.

The Messerschmitts astern were diving now, positioning themselves to get on the tails of Graham's four Spits, and Yeoman marvelled that the German pilots seemed to fall for the old trick every time.

'Break right!'

Once more the frantic merry-go-round, the sea twisting under the wings, the heavy, clutching hand of gravitational force as the Spitfires swung round to face the attackers. The Messerschmitts came in like sharks, fleeting and deadly, growing in size with terrifying speed.

There were six of them, and as the four Spitfires swung out of their turn the 109s split into two groups of three, skidding away to left and right.

The Spitfires split up too, Powell and McCallum chasing one group of 109s while Graham and Yeoman went after the others. The Messerschmitts were diving, heading inland at high speed towards Takali, silvery fish against the grey-green background, and Yeoman knew with a sudden flash of hopelessness that they had no chance of catching them, knew also that the 109s were decoys, that there must be more Huns up above, waiting to spring the trap.

Graham's Spitfire was still in a shallow dive, with Yeoman following. The altimeter wound down through twenty thousand feet. Flak was bursting all across the island, great dark flowerbeds of it at varying levels.

Yeoman craned his neck again, searching above, behind and to either side, and sure enough there they were, a cluster

54

of wasps streaming down out of the blue. He pressed the transmit button to warn Graham.

'Catfish Leader, Snappers five o'clock high, closing fast.'

'Righto, George, leave 'em. Big jobs nine o'clock, low. Let's go!'

Graham's Spitfire rolled over on its back and disappeared under Yeoman's port wing. Yeoman rolled too, feeling his seat harness tight on his shoulders as he pulled through, half-rolling again as the Spit's nose went down into a vertical dive, looking ahead for Graham and whatever it was that Graham was chasing.

He located Graham's fighter immediately, and a split second later sighted the target: a formation of about twenty Junkers 88 bombers, flying at fifteen thousand feet in three broad arrowheads.

Another glance back as he levelled out, a few hundred yards behind Graham, curving round for a beam attack on the leading formation of bombers: the Messerschmitts were still pouring down, gaining ground all the time.

To blazes with it! Ahead of him, Graham was already opening fire, grey smoke-trails streaming back from his wings. Yeoman selected a Ju 88 which was flying at a slightly lower altitude than the others and pushed the stick forward slightly, converging on it, firing as it leaped towards him. The Spitfire shuddered with the recoil of the cannon and the Junkers went into a sudden climbing turn. He fired again as his gunsight framed the bomber's nose and engines, seeing the big glasshouse cockpit shatter into a thousand sparkling slivers. The Junkers' wings, camouflaged in splinters of light and dark blue, loomed enormous in front of him as he loosed off a deflection shot inside its turn, glimpsing a vivid flash and a puff of smoke from one engine before his target whirled away and vanished.

Orange golf balls were flashing past his cockpit, just above his starboard wing, making a strange crackling noise that was clearly audible above the roar of the engine. He stared at them for a fraction of a second that stretched to infinity, mesmerized, then tore his eyes away and rammed the stick forward and to the left, diving away and looking back at the same time.

A hundred yards behind him was the head-on silhouette of another 88, its front gunner blazing away at him. The Spitfire lurched and he felt, rather than heard, a series of bangs somewhere behind the armour plating of his seat. He tightened the turn to the left, coming out of the dive and pulling up steeply, keeping the Junkers in sight all the time as it shot past. At the top of his climb he winged over, curving down to get on the bomber's tail.

He gave a quick glance around to check that he was in no immediate danger, then went after the JU 88 at full boost. The Junkers, its wings heavy with fat bombs and its dive-brakes fully open, was nosing down through twelve thousand feet over Rabat. Ahead, in the distance, more Junkers were diving on Luqa.

Yeoman overhauled the bomber quickly, ignoring the fireballs that flitted towards him from the 7.9-mm gun position at the rear of the bulbous cockpit. The tail unit and part of the rear fuselage crept into his sight. He made a small correction and the luminous dot of the sight moved a few degrees to the left, centring on the bomber's port engine.

The rear gunner was still firing, and Yeoman felt two more thumps as bullets struck the Spitfire. There was no time to worry about that now. The range was down to seventy-five yards and the bomber's dive was growing steeper. Yeoman stuck to it like a leech and jabbed his thumb down on the firing button.

His aim was good. There was a burst of white smoke and an instant later the engine blew apart, sending debris whirling back in the slipstream. A fuel tank in the wing exploded and a river of fire streamed past the bomber's tailplane. Yeoman gave a touch of right rudder and watched his shells flash across the 88's fuselage, striking the starboard engine. That, too, began to pour smoke.

One of the bomber's undercarriage legs suddenly fell down out of its housing, dangled uselessly for an instant, then broke off. Yeoman ducked as the assembly, wheel and all, skimmed over the top of his cockpit, missing him by a matter of feet.

The bomber was finished. Yeoman throttled back to avoid hitting the blazing mass, then turned away sharply as the enemy rear gunner, incredibly, opened fire once more. He had time only for one short burst, however, before the Junkers heeled over and plunged earthwards, spewing burning debris as it fell. It exploded a few thousand feet lower down in a soundless gush of smoke and flame. There had been no parachutes and Yeoman felt sorry for the German gunner. The man had shown plenty of guts; he had deserved to live.

Yeoman brought the Spitfire round in a tight turn, aware of the dangers of flying straight and level for more than a few seconds and looking round to get his bearings. The fight had carried him south and he was at five thousand feet over Dingli cliffs, on the coast to the west of Luqa. There was a lot of smoke rising from the airfield, and from Takali, but there was no sign of the bombers or, for that matter, of any aircraft at all. The grey-green smoke-screen over Grand Harbour was beginning to disperse, and the now-familiar reddish cloud of dust hung over the island like a malignant mushroom.

He wondered what had happened to the other Spitfires. He tried calling up Graham but his radio was completely dead, the set probably smashed when his aircraft was hit.

He looked at Luqa and Takali again. Both seemed to have been quite badly hit, and he decided not to attempt a landing on either. However, Safi strip, which was joined to Luqa by a series of rough taxiways, looked reasonably intact, and so did Hal Far, on the south coast.

He felt terribly uneasy. There was no flak, no aircraft, nothing. It was far too quiet. Also, there was too much haze at this height; anyone up above would be able to see him, but he would have difficulty in locating them.

His fuel was running low, and he felt a sudden overwhelming urge to set his fighter down, anywhere would do, any place where he might find people and overcome this awful

57

feeling of utter solitude. He turned towards Safi, and in that same heart-stopping flash of time he saw the 109s.

There were two of them, streaking in from the sea, their aggressive head-on silhouettes already twinkling with the flashes of their guns as they curved in towards Yeoman's Spitfire. Instinctively he turned towards them, catching a hazy impression of a third as it came at him from a different angle. He looked again for the first two but they had already vanished, their high speed carrying them a long way past after missing him with their first firing pass, but now two more were coming in from the right, cutting inside his turn.

Christ, they were coming at him from all sides! His hands on the stick were slippery and wet and sweat poured into his eyes, half blinding him. At all costs he had to keep turning; it was his only hope of salvation. With his radio dead there was no possibility of calling for help. He would have to sort out this predicament all by himself.

A Messerschmitt flashed under his nose, appearing ahead of him and entering his sight for a fraction of a second. He loosed off a rapid burst and the 109 flicked away sharply.

The two on his right were turning with him, aiming to cut him off, closing in for the kill. His arms ached with the effort of hauling the stick. He knew that he wasn't turning tightly enough, and increased the pressure, bringing the stick back into his stomach with the wings almost vertical, attempting the impossible.

The Spitfire protested, like a thoroughbred being forced at an unmanageable fence. A great tremble ran through her, and the next instant the sea was gyrating above Yeoman's head as she stalled out of the turn and went into a spin. Frantically, for he was now very low, Yeoman applied full rudder in the direction opposite to that of the spin's rotation and pushed the stick forward. The Spit responded beautifully and pulled out into a shallow dive, levelling out only feet above the rocky shoreline, the cliffs towering above her left wing.

Yeoman stayed low, keeping as close to the cliff as he dared. He was now safe from attack from one side, at least. A quick look up and behind revealed two Messerschmitts a few

58

thousand feet above the coast, waggling their wings; they seemed to have lost him.

Away to the right, Filfla island was a dark smudge on the horizon. Yeoman started to breathe again as his brain worked overtime to cope with his immediate problem and came up with a solution. With the Messerschmitts prowling over the island, apparently unopposed, there could be no question of attempting a landing at either Luqa or Safi. He would therefore keep as low as possible and follow the coast as it curved round to the south-east, leapfrogging the cliffs at the last moment to set his Spitfire down on Hal Far.

The two Messerschmitts were still with him, keeping pace. He realized that he must be in their blind spot, but that situation was only temporary. They were bound to spot him as soon as he pulled up over the cliffs.

He toyed with the notion of flying round the southern tip of the island and turning in towards Hal Far by way of Marsaxlokk Bay, but dismissed the idea almost immediately when he scanned his instruments: the oil pressure and temperature gauges were almost off the clock. An instant later, his worst fears were confirmed when smoke began to stream from under the engine cowling, and his ears detected a new, ominous note in the sound of the Merlin.

It was now or never. Pulling back the stick, he swept up over the crest of the cliff, skimming across the parched ground and dry stone walls, peering ahead to where Hal Far ought to be.

The smoke was denser now, obscuring his vision. He could hardly see a thing. He waggled his wings, looking for an open space, and at the same instant saw the two 109s racing down towards him. Jesus, he thought, I'm not going to make it.

The engine sounded like two skeletons making love on a tin roof. Suddenly, it seized altogether with a terrific crunch.

The smoke died away, and suddenly Yeoman could see again. Into his field of vision swept rutted taxiways, the charred skeletons of buildings. He spotted a clear patch of ground and side-slipped towards it, with stick fully back and full top rudder. There was no time to lower the undercart, and with this pitted surface it would probably have proved fatal anyway.

He levelled out and the Spitfire floated for an eternity, the ground blurring beneath her wings. Dead ahead, a huge bomb crater loomed out of the landscape; Yeoman ruddered hard to miss it and found himself confronted by another obstacle, the remains of a stone wall.

He almost closed his eyes in despair. Nothing mattered now but sheer naked instinct. He pulled the stick back, knowing that he was going to hit the wall but pulling it back anyway in a last, desperate attempt to cushion the inevitable impact. Time stood still, and for a weird moment it seemed as though he were outside the cockpit, looking down on himself. Strange thoughts passed through his mind. In a detached sort of way, he wondered how he was going to die; whether his head would smash into the gunsight and burst open like a rotten apple, or whether his body would be pierced in a dozen places by slivers of jagged metal when the cockpit burst apart.

The Spitfire struck the wall tail-down with a bone-jarring crunch, sending masonry and white dust flying in all directions. Yeoman put his arms up in front of his face as the brutal deceleration slammed him forward in his straps. The fighter slewed across the dry ground, skidding violently as a wingtip struck a heap of rubble, shedding fragments of metal, and came to a stop a few feet from a shattered stone hut.

There was a heavy silence, broken only by a metallic crackling sound from the dead engine.

Yeoman, dazed and stunned, slowly became aware of his surroundings. Still in slow motion, or so it seemed, he reached up to open the cockpit hood and found to his amazement that it was already open. He couldn't remember having opened it.

He pulled off his helmet, unfastened his straps and tried to stand up, only to flop back down again. He placed both hands on the cockpit rail and tried again, heaving himself upright,

60

standing on his parachute pack. His legs were trembling and unsteady.

There was something he had forgotten. Frowning, his brain still dulled he tried to remember what it was.

The Messerschmitts. Christ, the Messerschmitts!

He tumbled out of the cockpit on to the crumpled remains of the wing, sliding off it into the dust, searching frantically for some shelter. He saw a bomb crater thirty yards away and stumbled towards it, still dazed and staggering.

The Messerschmitts were coming for him, to murder him, personally, sweeping down in a strident whistling snarl of engines. He tripped over some stones and fell headlong into the crater, bruising himself painfully, and covered his head with his arms.

Hal Far's Bofors opened up with a noise like thousands of hammers beating on metal drums. Shrapnel hissed through the air, raining down like sleet on the surface of the airfield. The noise of engines rose to a terrific crescendo, mingled briefly with a staccato banging of cannon and machine-guns, then faded.

Gradually, the volume of anti-aircraft fire decreased until the Bofors fell silent. Cautiously, spitting out dust, Yeoman raised his head above the lip of the crater.

A few yards away, wisps of smoke rose from the wreck of his Spitfire, which was riddled with holes. Beyond it, he saw what looked like an ambulance, lurching across the field towards him.

He clambered out of the crater and sat down weakly on a mound of stones. For the first time in his life, he felt a desperate craving for a cigarette.

Chapter Five

Yeoman rubbed a hand wearily over his eyes. The bombers had been over Malta in strength again that night, and no one had got much sleep.

He sighed, and stared at the handwritten words in front of him. Although it was forbidden by the regulations, he had decided to keep a diary of his experiences on Malta. If he came through—and just at this moment he didn't rate his chances very highly—it would provide an invaluable source of reference when, one day, he came to write about the conflict of which he was a tiny part; if he did not, then others would read it and know at least part of the truth.

Looking at what he had written now, the words seemed alien, as though they had been set down by and described the experiences of someone else. What he had written was really an introduction to the diary proper, a condensation of what he had seen and done, a catalogue of his impressions during the eighteen days he had spent on the island so far.

Eighteen days! Writing down today's date at the head of the first page—Wednesday, 27 May—had come almost as a physical shock. Time had ceased to have any meaning since that first hectic action of 10 May; life itself had been an endless cycle of flying, fighting and sleeping, with hasty meals thrown in between whenever the opportunity arose. He recalled arriving back at Luqa after that crashlanding at Hal Far, when the expressions on the faces of the 'old hands' had left him with the distinct feeling that if they could have chosen between himself and the Spitfire returning intact, their choice would have been the fighter. And no wonder, with seven more of the island's vital Spitfires and Hurricanes destroyed that day. Even though the defenders had shot down fifteen enemy aircraft, the rate of attrition was still far too high.

Sergeant McCallum had died that day. Pursued by 109s, he had made for Takali and, following instructions, had dropped down inside the ring of anti-aircraft guns. It had made no difference; the Messerschmitts had swooped and Mac's Spitfire had crashed upside down and exploded in the middle of the airfield.

Suddenly, Yeoman wished that he was an artist. That was the true way to capture the contrasts of Malta; the golden light of the island's central plain, sweeping down from the higher ground in the north to the deep anchorages of Grand Harbour through ancient towns whose names sounded like clarions through centuries of ravelled history: Birkirkara, Hamrun, Floriana and finally Valletta itself, where the Knights of Malta had defied the Turks; the gold and ivory pastel shades of churches and cathedrals, their spires a glory against the blue of sea and sky. There was a kind of beauty, too, in the darting, twisting aircraft that played like shoals of fish over the island, their wings glinting in the sun, in the multi-coloured flak-bursts that blossomed and drifted and evaporated.

And then the horror and the fear, the stench and the dust and the flies. The fearful stomach cramps that accompanied the Malta Dog, the nausea and the vomiting and the diarrhoea, the panic-stricken sweating of face and palms that accompanied the endless wait before each alert. The continual discomfort; the freezing cold at twenty-eight thousand feet, the muscles that ached from the strain of hurling one's fighter around the sky, almost always on the defensive, the utter weariness, the ever-present knowledge that there was nowhere to hide from the bombs and the strafing fighters and that the next sortie might be one's last, the dreadful feeling of lassitude and weakness and anticlimax when one got down safely each time.

The words swam in front of Yeoman's eyes. He had tried to capture everything, all the disjointed impressions of beauty and horror. An old Maltese couple, working unconcernedly on their patch of barren earth close by the airfield perimeter as the sirens wailed, looking up briefly and waving to him as he taxied past in his Spitfire. The dusty, ragged girl in Naxxar, seizing his hand and pressing her worn prayer card into it. (Although far from religious he carried it with him constantly, in his shirt pocket.) The Junkers 88s, howling down over Rabat towards the smoke cloud that hung over Takali, some dropping their bombs short so that they plunged into the town. The fallen masonry choking the streets, the merciful shroud of white dust hiding the human debris. An occasional glimpse of something bloody and inhuman on a stretcher.

The pilot, one of the old Malta hands, all of twenty-two years old, twitching and screaming, running naked from the billets in Naxxar in broad daylight and blowing out his brains with his Service revolver because he couldn't take any more.

The broken debris of aircraft, strewn around the perimeter of the airfields, skeletal in the sunshine. The burning wreckage of Junkers and Messerschmitts and Spitfires and Hurricanes and Macchis, spiralling earthwards. Parachutes, shining in the sun, drifting through the clusters of flak. The airmen, burned dark brown by the sun, toiling ceaselessly, always grumbling yet paradoxically always cheerful.

The faces that vanished from the Mess with each new day, some known, some nameless.

It was all so jumbled. Yet this was Malta in May 1942: a crazy jigsaw puzzle in which none of the pieces quite fitted together, a kaleidoscope of whirling events that robbed a man of any delusion that he was in control of his own destiny. You flew and you fought and you hit the enemy whenever you had the chance, and if you were lucky you got back. Sometimes you were very lucky, and caught the bombers without a fighter escort. Like those eight Italian Cant z 1007s the other day, for example. He searched for his account of the action among the scrawled words, and re-read it.

21 May. Several false alarms this morning. Eventually scrambled at noon with four Spits. Graham, self, Powell, Wilcox. Joined by two Hurricanes from Hal Far. Douggie ordered us to climb to Angels thirty over Gozo. Visibility perfect, with Sicily clearly visible. Spotted the Italians almost at once, in beautiful formation; two 'diamonds' of four aircraft. There wasn't a fighter in sight except our own. Came in from astern in pairs. Enemy took no evasive action whatsoever. I was conscious of how beautiful the enemy bombers were; elegant and streamlined, so different from the angular Junkers 88s. Long, slender fuselages, three engines and twin fins. Closed with the machine on the extreme left of the second formation, fired short burst. Thin smoke-trail from his starboard engine. Dived under him, dodging fire from his ventral gunner. Gerry Powell finished him off.

Attacked rearmost aircraft of leading formation. Noted odd camouflage, all mottled greens, browns and greys, with Italian insignia standing out boldly. Closed in to less than 100 yards; first burst blew chunks off his starboard fin, second set starboard engine on fire. Enemy aircraft went down in shallow diving turn to port and I followed. Next burst set port engine on fire and e/a's dive steepened until almost vertical. Enemy aircraft hit ground near Qala (Gozo) and blew up. Observed two parachutes. Remainder of enemy formation totally destroyed, five by our chaps, rest by Hurricanes from Hal Far. One Hurri hit by return fire and ditched; pilot OK and picked up by ASR, together with half a dozen Italians.

The z 1007 was Yeoman's second kill since his arrival in Malta; his only other claim was one Junkers 88 damaged. Gerry Powell's score already stood at three Messerschmitt

109s, one Macchi 202 and a Ju 88, in addition to the z 1007 he had destroyed, while Roger Graham had knocked down three Ju 88s.

Yeoman picked up his pencil, pondered for a few moments, then wrote:

It rained yesterday, which is unusual for this time of year. A great towering black storm-cloud built up over the island, all purple-black and grey, outlined in silver by the sun. There was no alert and we sat on the ground and watched a few 109s skimming round its edges, like minnows in a pond, but they didn't come down and left us in peace. There was hardly any action during the day, but the enemy made up for it last night. Valletta again, and some bombs on Hal Far too. We're all bog-eyed this morning—a hell of a start to our forty-eight hour leave.

The chair creaked as Yeoman sat back and stretched, laying down his pencil and closing his notebook. Leave! He chuckled inwardly. That was a laugh. Gerry Powell and he had arranged to spend their precious forty-eight hours in Valletta, and it would probably be a damn' sight more dangerous there than at Luqa. Still, at least they would have two whole days free of the nerve-racking strain of waiting for alerts, of the sheer physical drain of flying four or five sorties a day.

'C'mon, George, we gotta be going. We're wasting valuable floozie time.'

Yeoman looked up and grinned as Powell came into the room. The Canadian was wearing his best uniform and positively glowed with anticipation of hitting the fleshpots of Valletta like a mini-tornado.

'Don't panic, Gerry,' Yeoman said. 'There's still fifteen minutes to bus time, and it's always late. Anyway, I'm ready now.'

He put away his diary and picked up a blue canvas bag containing a change of clothing and his shaving kit. Then, taking a last look round to make sure he hadn't forgotten

66

anything, he followed Powell along the corridor, down the stone staircase and out into the morning sunlight.

It was just after nine o'clock, but already Naxxar's small square was dancing with heat. They sat down to await the bus on the steps of the church, taking some comfort from the shade and watching the friendly, chattering Maltese people going about their business. Yeoman and Powell were not the only ones heading for Valletta, as the minutes ticked by a small crowd began to gather. It was composed mainly of civilians, Maltese workmen with their inevitable coating of white dust, but there were also three or four more RAF types from the Takali Wing. Yeoman didn't recognize them, although he knew that they must have been sharing the same building for some time.

By nine-thirty the crowd was beginning to show signs of impatience, with the volume of chatter increasing. The bus was already twenty minutes late and it only had to come from Mosta, a mile or so up the road.

'Excuse me, sir.'

Yeoman looked up, startled. The man had appeared from nowhere. He was small and dark-skinned, wizened by years of sun, and wore a khaki uniform of sorts. His shoulder flashes proclaimed that he was a member of the Royal Malta Artillery. He saluted smartly.

'You are waiting for the bus, sir?' he asked, beaming in a friendly fashion. Yeoman agreed that they were.

The soldier's smile disappeared and he shook his head sadly. 'It will not come, sir,' he told the pilots. 'I, Joseph Grech, know that it will not come, for the husband of my sister, Tony Camilleri, is its driver, and he is very sick.'

Powell rolled his eyes heavenwards. 'Oh, bloody hell!' he exclaimed. Yeoman looked at the diminutive Grech. 'You are sure about this?' he queried.

The soldier spread his hands, as though in apology. 'Quite sure, sir,' he answered. 'The bus will not come today.'

Some of the people in the small crowd had overheard his words, and those who understood English were starting to drift away.

'Well,' Yeoman said to Powell, 'there's no point in hanging around here. Looks as though we'll have to hoof it.'

Grech brought himself to attention, stiffening to the full height of his five feet four inches, and announced, dramatically:

'Sirs, you will not need to walk. In a few minutes a truck of the Royal Malta Artillery'—he pronounced the words with a proud ring in his voice—'will arrive, driven by my corporal, Angus Sultana. It is going as far as Hamrun. I myself will arrange for you to have a lift.'

Yeoman thanked Grech, who glowed with pride, and grinned to himself, wondering about Angus Sultana's parentage. In fact, the man turned out to be a larger version of Grech, who spoke to him volubly in Maltese, explaining the sad business of Tony Camilleri, husband of his sister, who was sick, and who therefore was unable to drive the daily bus into Valletta, which therefore would not now arrive.

The corporal stuck his head out of the window of the dust-caked truck and grinned toothlessly at Yeoman. 'Awright, sir,' he said.

'Awright, Corporal,' Yeoman answered. He was beginning to pick up bits of Maltese. For generations, British troops and sailors had been greeting the inhabitants of Malta with the traditional salutation. 'All right, Johnny?', and the corrupted version had infiltrated into the language until it had become the accepted word for 'hello'.

Grech offered the RAF officers a seat in the cab of the truck but they declined, indicating that it was the little soldier's rightful place. He radiated pleasure and got inside. Yeoman, Powell and the airmen from Takali clambered into the back and squatted down on the floor. Like everything else, it was coated with white powder.

'Bang goes our best khaki,' Powell said ruefully.

'It'll brush off,' Yeoman replied. 'Anyway, it's better than walking.'

The last was a fatal pronouncement, as he discovered a few minutes later. Sultana took the truck careering through the narrow streets of Naxxar as though all the devils in hell were in hot pursuit, increasing speed still more as the vehicle burst out on to the hot, dusty road that led down over the open plain towards Birkirkara. At one point it hit a massive rut and almost turned over, throwing the occupants into a heap in the middle of the floor. Yeoman's head came into violent contact with the midriff of one of the Takali pilots, a bull-necked flight sergeant, and both men treated themselves to a bout of fluent cursing as they sorted themselves out.

'Mind you,' said the flight sergeant, 'it might be uncomfortable, but it's the only way to travel around these parts. You often get 109s cruising round the island in between raids, and they'll shoot at anything that moves. You're a sitting duck, out here in the open. They shot up a bus load of schoolkids the other day, and killed half a dozen of them.'

On this occasion the Messerschmitts were fortunately absent, and Sultana's driving remained the only hazard confronting the truck's passengers. Yeoman, clinging on grimly, peered over the tailboard through the cloud of swirling dust, catching brief glimpses of the landscape as it swept past. They swayed and jolted through Birkirkara, with its cluster of white, flat-roofed houses; Yeoman remembered that there was an army barracks here, and that it had recently been bombed with considerable loss of life. Small villages appeared and then vanished just as quickly behind the dust-cloud as the truck sped on, and then suddenly they were passing through the arches of an aqueduct and Yeoman looked around him with renewed interest as buildings appeared on either side.

The truck slowed appreciably as it entered Hamrun, for the streets of the ancient town were heavily congested. The engine whined as Sultana changed gear, slithered round a hairpin bend and took the vehicle up a short but steep hill. At the top he pulled off the road and stopped, switching off the engine.

The passengers climbed down gratefully, dusting themselves down, and gazed at their surroundings. The truck was parked by the edge of what appeared to be ornamental gardens of some sort—or at least that is what they might have been, before the army took over. They were now the site of a battery of anti-aircraft guns, their long barrels pointing skywards at an angle over the city of Floriana towards the deepwater inlets of Grand Harbour.

Grech came round to the rear of the truck and saluted. He said, apologetically:

'This is as far as we can take you, sirs. In any case, no vehicle can pass through Floriana. The streets are completely blocked.'

'That's all right,' Yeoman replied, 'we can easily walk from here. I'd like to thank you and Corporal Sultana for your help. Good luck to you.'

'It was a pleasure, sir,' the little man said. 'And if you come to Mosta, come also to the Union Bar. It is owned by the cousin of my sister-in-law, and there you will always be welcome.'

Yeoman nodded and smiled, thanking Grech, then set off down the road with Powell into Floriana.

'It's a bit puzzling,' Powell exclaimed suddenly. Yeoman looked at him questioningly. 'What is?' he asked.

'The little feller's family ties,' his companion grinned. 'He seems to have brothers and cousins and sisters-in-law all over the place. Still, the Union Bar might be worth visiting. You never know—sister-in-law might be a respectable bit of crumpet.'

'Fat and fifty, more like,' Yeoman grunted. 'Anyway, you want to watch your step with this lot. Start mucking about with their nearest and dearest, and you're liable to get a stiletto up your backside.'

Floriana was a shambles. It was as though the old city had been systematically smashed to pieces, street by street, with a giant hammer. The buildings, constructed in the main from blocks of soft limestone, had proved completely incapable of withstanding bomb blast; the shock waves had crushed them like eggs, choking the streets with mountains of collapsed masonry.

The pilots picked their way through the stone wilderness, past gangs of Maltese workmen labouring under a dusty shroud to clear a road through the rubble. Miraculously, they appeared to be succeeding, at least in part; as Yeoman and Powell walked on, the narrow track between the shattered houses broadened steadily until it became a recognizable roadway, wide enough to allow the passage of transport. They stuck carefully to the middle of it, for here there were many empty shells of buildings on either side, their walls cracked and leaning at all sorts of odd angles. One of them, taller than the rest, caught Yeoman's attention and he stopped, gazing at it in fascination. Its outside walls had crumbled away completely, stripped off by some mysterious trick of blast, but the walls of the rooms inside were still intact. It looked like a house of cards, capped crazily by what was left of the roof. Broken and splintered furniture was still inside, piled haphazardly into the corners, and here and there a torn lace curtain fluttered, caught in a jagged tangle of stone.

'I wonder who lived there,' Yeoman said, voicing his thoughts aloud.

'Well,' Powell retorted, 'whoever it was they certainly aren't living there now. Come on, for Christ's sake, before the bloody place falls down on us. Besides, I'm parched.'

They turned into a narrow lane, a defile sliced through the living rock that plunged steeply down towards the harbour. It was shady here, and the doors and windows of houses gaped at them, dark caverns of gloom in which one sensed movement. The bombs had done their work here, too, as scattered blocks of stone and pock-marked walls testified, but most of the buildings were still intact, the depth of the street having sheltered them from the worst of the onslaught. As the pilots descended towards the rectangle of light that marked the far end of the alley they encountered growing numbers of people, most of them converging on a single shop outside of which black-clad women stood in a long queue, waiting patiently. The whole shop front was open to the street and Yeoman peered in as they went past, catching a glimpse of an enormously fat woman weighing rations on a pair of iron scales. Some of her customers glanced with brief curiosity at the two men, then looked away disinterestedly. Yeoman was reminded of the 'business as usual' signs outside battered shops in London's bombed-out East End during the blitz, and of the 'London can take it' slogans chalked on the walls. Malta was taking it, too, with magnificent courage, and Yeoman felt a sudden great surge of affection for her dauntless people.

They emerged into the sunlight at the far end of the street and turned on to what had once been an avenue. It was still lined with the blast-shattered remnants of trees. It had become the main thoroughfare between Floriana and Valletta, for the main road that ran parallel to it was completely blocked by rubble, piled fifteen feet high in some places. Beyond the rubble was a stone wall, with great gaps torn in it. The pilots picked their way across to it and stood at one of the gaps, looking down into one of the deep inlets of the harbour.

'God,' muttered Yeoman, appalled by what he saw. 'What an awful bloody mess.'

It was like a scene from the Apocalypse, a vista of utter devastation. The dockside was a nightmare jungle of shattered warehouses, with the jibs of cranes protruding here and there at crazy angles, while the harbour itself was choked with sunken and capsized ships, their masts, funnels and rusting hulls breaking the smooth surface of the water.

The sight was not new to Yeoman; he had seen something similar in the Libyan port of Tobruk a year earlier. But this was infinitely worse, a graveyard of ships that left him with a leaden feeling of horror.

He moved his gaze quickly away from the tangle of wreckage, looking across the inlet to where the town of Senglea nestled on its clifftop. Its walls were a gentle yellow-white in the sun against the deep blue of the sky, a relief to the eye after the carnage over which it presided. It seemed to be intact, an oasis of peace amid the murderous aftermath of the raids, but Yeoman knew that this was no more than an illusion; Senglea was a broken shell of a town, its buildings torn and crumbled with the same ferocity that had levelled Floriana.

'Come on,' he said to Powell, 'let's go. I could do with a drink myself, now.'

They walked on in silence for a few minutes, then Yeoman said thoughtfully: 'It makes you wonder, seeing a mess like that. Whether we're doing our job, I mean. Whether we're shooting enough of the bastards down.'

'Oh, we're shooting them down all right,' replied Powell, 'but don't forget that we're looking at the results of nearly two years of raids. And we're on a shoestring all the time. If we could put up sixty or seventy Spits and Hurricanes each time, instead of nine or ten, it would be a different story.'

He paused, then looked directly at Yeoman. 'Do you really think we can stop them, George, if they tried to invade?'

Yeoman shrugged. 'I only wish I could answer that question,' he said, 'but I just don't know. We could have stopped 'em in Crete, if we'd had enough fighters; that I do know. It all depends on whether we can keep the reinforcements and supplies coming in, and that depends on the Navy. They'll do their job, if it's humanly possible. After that, it's up to us. If we can only establish air superiority—I don't mean in numerical terms, but if we can shoot enough of the sods down every time they come over to make them think twice—then they won't come. The Jerries don't like water, and Crete must have frightened the daylights out of them. They really took a hammering in the early stages, from what I saw. No, you can be certain of one thing; the dice will have to be very heavily loaded in their favour before they'll risk invading.'

'Well, I only hope you're right,' Powell grunted. 'I just wish we had some idea of how long it's going to go on, that's all. At the moment, it's a toss-up who gets us first, the Jerries or the Dog.'

'Yes,' said Yeoman, 'I've been lucky there, all right. No sign of the Dog at all so far, touch wood, apart from the odd twinge. Poor old Roger Graham's latest bout was really

73

'nasty; I thought I was going to have to take over the squadron for another few days, at one point.'

'Instead of which,' Powell grinned, 'here you are, nicely off the hook and bound for a couple of days' debauchery. If we can find any among this lot,' he added as an afterthought, looking round at the sea of destruction.

'I'm not really bothered about that,' Yeoman answered. 'I'd rather see what's left of the sights, meet a few of the people.'

'God, George, what an awful bloody liar you are!' Powell gave a guffaw of laughter. 'I'm keen to meet a few of the people, too, but there are a couple of conditions—they've got to be female, and they've got to be horizontal at the time.'

They skirted the debris of a collapsed house and found themselves on the main street of Floriana again, where it curved round to join the avenue. Ahead of them the street split in two and they took the left fork, heading for the great gateway that led on to Kingsway, the main artery of Valletta. The right-hand fork curved up a slope towards St. Michael's Square; on the far side of the square was the long tunnel that led on to the RAF's main operations room, from which Group Captain Douglas and his hard-worked team of controllers directed Malta's fighter defences. The back door of the ops room opened on to Strait Street, the deep alley that sliced to the harbour through sheer rock. To the countless British service men who had discovered a few minutes' dubious delight in the arms of the prostitutes who infested it, Strait Street was more popularly known as The Gut.

The two pilots passed under the ancient archway and stopped, looking down the road. Kingsway dropped away sharply for a few hundred yards, then climbed steeply again. Its whole length was littered with rubble.

They began to move forward down the slope. After a few paces, Yeoman stopped and grabbed Powell's arm.

'Just a sec,' he said, a note of urgency in his voice. 'Have you noticed anything?'

'No, what is it? I don't see anything.'

74

'That's just it. There aren't any people about. There should be droves of them at this time of day. It's almost as if—'

The wail of a siren, its note rising and falling, cut through his words. A few moments later they heard the roar of aero-engines, reverberating from the walls around them.

Yeoman started to run, propelling Powell towards a mound of rubble that stood beside a low wall, all that remained of some bombed-out building.

'Just as I thought,' he shouted breathlessly, as they sprinted across the street, their shoes kicking up spurts of dust. 'The Maltese seem to have a sixth sense about when there's a raid coming in. They must have all legged it for the shelters minutes ago.'

They threw themselves into the narrow gap between the rubble and the stone wall, crouching in the dust, their ears battered by the note of the sirens and the swelling throb of engines. Somewhere behind the ruined buildings, anti-aircraft guns opened up.

Yeoman tilted his head to one side, trying in vain to establish the direction of the incoming aircraft. The noise of their motors bounced around the street, echoing from wall to wall. The bark of the anti-aircraft guns intensified until it became a continuous roll of sound.

An engine howled stridently, accompanied by the rending screech of a Stuka's underwing sirens. Every nerve in Yeoman's body screamed at him to lie prone and cover his head with his hands, following Powell's example, but he went on searching for the source of the noise. He caught a fleeting glimpse of a gull-winged shape, flashing past a gap in the buildings on the far side of the street as the Stuka pulled out of its dive, very low. An instant later, the earth heaved under him as the aircraft's bomb exploded, some-where out of sight. Stones clattered from the ruined build-ings, bouncing across the street.

The sky was filled with the shriek of engines, the whistle and thump of bombs. He ducked as a great cloud of dust and smoke erupted halfway down the street, a couple of hundred yards away. This time the concussion was fearsome, stun-

75

ning him. Blast waves rippled across the ground, plucking at his protective pile of stones. Beside him, Powell let out a sudden cry and tried to get up; Yeoman pushed him flat again, holding him down with an outstretched arm.

'The shelter!' Powell cried, choking on dust. 'Got to get to the shelter!'

'We'd never make it,' Yeoman yelled in his ear. 'Too far! Past where that last bomb went off!'

Their world dissolved in a wave of noise that lasted for a few seconds or an eternity. The walls of Valletta captured the hellish din of diving Stukas and amplified it, magnifying it tenfold. The sun vanished behind boiling clouds of smoke. Dust drifted along the street, settling and covering everything, clogging eyes and nostrils.

The silence that followed was oppressive, the kind of silence that follows a mortal hurt before the victim realizes, and screams. The age-old walls of the city still trembled, as though Valletta was weeping inwardly, sobbing with the injury and injustice of it, as though to say: I have weathered centuries of storms, storms made by the men I have seen come and go across the sea. This is the worst of all, for my very heart is being destroyed. No more, I beg, no more!

The two pilots got up, spitting out grit and dusting themselves down as best they could. Slowly, without speaking, they made their way down Kingsway, skirting the still-smoking bomb crater.

The all-clear had not yet sounded, but already people were beginning to emerge from their holes in the ground and go about their business as though nothing had happened. The bomb that had fallen on Kingsway did not seem to have inflicted any casualties, but in the distance Yeoman could hear the rumble of falling masonry, and it did not take much imagination to visualize the rescue teams working frantically to release people entombed under fresh mounds of rubble.

A few yards past the bomb crater they came to the entrance of an air-raid shelter. The faint murmur of voices drifted from the dark interior. The sound had a rhythmic quality to it and Yeoman, his curiosity aroused, went into the entrance.

Powell, his thirst still uppermost in his mind, rolled his eyes heavenwards in despair and then followed him.

A long tunnel curved down through the rock, lit by the occasional electric bulb, its walls glistening with damp. The stench that floated up it was nauseating; a compound of sweat, burnt fat, human excrement and a dozen other subtler and less definable odours. Yeoman gagged and almost turned back, but his curiosity overcame him and he forced himself to go on. Gerry Powell's stomach, already severely upset, dictated otherwise: muttering 'See you in a minute', he beat a hasty retreat back up the tunnel.

The murmur grew in volume. The tunnel curved sharply, and Yeoman suddenly found himself standing on a kind of raised dais. Steps led down from it to the floor of a large cavern. The rhythmic chanting was loud and echoing now, rolling from wall to wall, cutting through the foul air.

It was a few seconds before Yeoman's eyes grew accustomed to the shadowy gloom, and the tableau that gradually pieced itself together was, to him at least, extraordinary.

There must have been at least two hundred people—men, women and children—in the cavern, all kneeling in prayer, facing a solitary priest who held a crucifix high above his head. They were saying their rosary, their words loud and confident.

Yeoman shivered, and suddenly felt very humble. This, then, must be what men called Faith: the spiritual shield which these people, in their simplicity, believed would protect them from the enemy bombs. This was why Malta and her people had endured through all their centuries of turmoil, and doubtless why they would endure for centuries to come.

He recalled the story of the thousand-pound bomb that had penetrated the dome of the cathedral in Mosta, when over a thousand people were praying inside. It had bounced up the aisle, missing them all, and come to rest against the far wall without exploding. If that wasn't divine intervention, then what was?

Come on, George, he told himself, pulling himself

together, it was more likely the result of some German armourer not doing his job properly. Nevertheless, he went back up the tunnel very slowly and quietly, so as not to disturb the strange congregation. Despite himself he felt horribly guilty, as though he had made an inexcusable intrusion into someone's deepest privacy.

Powell was waiting for him at the entrance, showing every sign of impatience.

'Thought you'd gone to sleep down there,' he said. 'What's going on, anyway?'

'Oh, just a lot of people praying,' Yeoman told him.

'Well, I hope they put in a request for a few more Spits while they're at it. Meantime, I'm praying for two things. First a drink, then a floozie. There's a bar just down the road; it must be in business, because I've seen folks going in and out. C'mon, let's give it a try.'

Belatedly, the all-clear sounded as they entered the bar. It was small and gloomy, but the proprietor—a small, rotund man in a spotless white shirt and dark trousers—looked up from his task of wiping a layer of dust from the tables as they came in and grinned at them in a friendly fashion. They grinned back, but stopped grinning abruptly when he told them that there was only one drink in the house, and that was goat's milk.

He urged them to try it and they accepted reluctantly—to find themselves pleasantly surprised. The milk was cool, with a strange, subtle flavour which they discovered was almond. It slaked their thirst beautifully, and they ordered another before leaving. The proprietor refused to accept any payment, insisting only that they return sometime to meet the rest of his family. Feeling faintly embarrassed, they thanked him and went out into the sunlight.

'We'll get the Dog now for sure,' Powell commented morosely as they walked on. 'They feed the grass with shit, then feed the grass to the goats. We've just been drinking liquid shit. The goat was just the middleman, that's all.'

Yeoman burst out laughing. 'You're a cheerful old bastard, and no mistake,' he said. 'I haven't tasted anything nicer for a long time. Anyway, I didn't notice—'

He broke off suddenly as something tugged insistently at his sleeve. He looked down. A small and very dirty walnut-coloured boy was grinning up at him.

'Pennies, Johnny,' a small voice piped.

Yeoman smiled. He reached into his trouser pocket and drew out a handful of coins.

The next instant there were children everywhere, bursting out of doorways, leaping from behind piles of rubble. They surrounded the pilots, laughing and chattering, jumping up and down in their excitement.

'Pennies, Johnny, pennies, Johnny,' they chanted in unison.

Yeoman raised his arms, sent the coins scattering across the street in a glittering arc. The children fell on them like a pack of starving dogs.

'Come on,' he said to his companion, 'let's get out of here!'

They ran off down the street. Yeoman risked a glance behind; the children had gathered up the money and were in hot pursuit, yelping wildly.

The pilots veered off Kingsway into a narrow, rutted street. They spotted an open doorway and dived in, flattening their bodies into the shadows. Moments later the frenzied mob of children went howling past, their bare feet pattering.

Powell wiped his brow. 'Jeez,' he said, 'give me the bombs, any time.'

Yeoman made no reply. There was a hand on his thigh, squeezing gently. He swung round, startled.

A woman was staring up at him, grinning toothlessly. The front of her tattered blouse was open and her half-exposed breasts flopped in an untidy heap over her waistline. She couldn't have been more than thirty years old.

'Hello, Johnny,' she lisped. 'You got some money for me?'

'Christ!' gasped Yeoman.

They fled.

Chapter Six

Captain Joachim Richter yawned, lifted the flap of his flying helmet, and massaged a large and painful carbuncle on his right cheek. He made the ritual scan of the instrument panel and brought the throttle back ever so slightly, adjusting the engine revs.

He looked around him, at the Messerschmitt 109s strung out across the sky. There were twenty-eight of them, including his own, the full complement of the 1st and 2nd Squadrons of Fighter Wing 66.

Richter was weary. It had been a long flight from Nikolayev, in the Ukraine; over eleven hundred miles, with nothing but the heavy silence of the engine's roar and the dancing of the needles on the instrument panel for company. The other Messerschmitts seemed as remote as the moon, even though there was only a couple of hundred metres between each aircraft. In a single-seat fighter, when radio silence was imposed, you were completely isolated from your fellow men.

They had stopped three times to refuel and stretch their legs: first at Bucharest, then at Skopje in Yugoslavia, and finally at Crotone, on the south-west tip of the Gulf of Taranto. From there they had flown across the 'toe' of Italy, crossing the coast on a south-westerly heading high above the Straits of Messina. Now, at last, they were approaching their destination, the Sicilian airfield of Catania, lying in the shadow of Mount Etna.

Yes, it had been a long flight; but, by God, every mile had been worth it. Every mile that put more distance between them and Russia, that accursed wilderness that swallowed men up contemptuously, without trace.

Eleven months they had been there, right from the start of Operation Barbarossa in June 1941. Eleven stinking months, roasting in the summer, soaked through and mudcaked in the autumn, freezing to death in the winter.

The winter! Although it was warm in the cockpit Richter shivered. He never wanted to experience anything like that again. Even huddled round the stove in the peasant's hut that served as the officers' mess, they had never managed to keep warm—and they had been the lucky ones. The real sufferers had been the front-line soldiers of the Wehrmacht, holding their positions out there on the steppes. There had been hardly any winter clothing; someone's head should certainly roll for that. He had seen the frozen bodies of soldiers who had died at their posts around the airfield perimeter, still standing stiffly in their foxholes, glazed, ice-rimmed eyes staring out over the wastelands, rifles clenched in frostbitten hands.

It had been different in the beginning, just like a field-day, almost.

They had practically wiped out the Soviet Air Force in those early weeks of the campaign, shooting down the tubby little I-16 Rata fighters, the SB-2 bombers, the Shturmovik ground-attack aircraft in their dozens. He himself had destroyed nine Russian aircraft in a single day, five of them on one sortie. They had been twin-engined SB-2s—'Katyushas', the Russians called them. They had just sat there, in perfect formation, making no attempt at evasive action, while he shot them down in flames one after the other. Only one enemy gunner had returned his fire.

The winter had brought an end to the Luftwaffe's orgy of destruction. Determined though the men had been to maintain the air offensive, it was impossible to fly in the teeth of a raging blizzard, or in sub-zero temperatures where even engine oil froze solid. The army had reached the gates of

Moscow, had pushed on through the Ukraine towards the vital oilfields of the Caucasus, but the onset of winter had put an effective brake on further progress and had brought the Reds the respite they so desperately needed.

During the winter months, intelligence reports had indicated that the Russians had moved entire factories to the east, beyond the Ural mountains where no German bomber could reach them, and had been churning out aircraft and tanks by the thousand. No one had seriously believed the reports at the time, least of all the Wehrmacht High Command, but the pack of lies had turned out to be true, because with the spring thaw the Soviet Air Force had begun to appear over the front in growing strength and Russian tanks, particularly armoured monsters known as T-34s, had been thrown into the battle on an unprecedented scale. Although a new German offensive in the south-east was pushing on towards the Caucasus, it was steadily losing momentum as its lines of communication became overstretched, and further north it was virtually stalemate.

God knows what the rest of 1942 will bring, mused Richter. One thing was certain: there would be no more easy victories in Russia. His tour on the eastern front had brought his score up to fifty-one enemy aircraft destroyed, all of them confirmed. It was a lot by anyone's standard, but many Luftwaffe fighter pilots had achieved far more. The score of eighty achieved by the First World War ace, Baron Manfred von Richthofen, had already been passed by a handsome margin by the young men of a different generation.

Richter was glad he had seen the first months of the Russian campaign, not just because they had enabled him to increase his score, but because they had furnished him with valuable experience as a tactical fighter leader, flying in support of the army. He had no doubt that it would come in useful, one day. Meanwhile, he was completely honest with himself; wild horses wouldn't drag him back to Russia. He was quite happy to be where he was, right now, even though there had been no home leave. There would be plenty of time for that later, when they had the Mediterranean business all sewn up.

They were approaching the Sicilian coast now, and the leading squadron of Messerschmitts was beginning to descend. Richter's squadron followed suit, dropping down towards the plain on which Catania airfield stood, flanked by mountains on both sides. Visibility was perfect and the view breathtaking, the scene dominated by the great cone of Etna. The Messerschmitts passed close to the giant volcano as they positioned themselves to land. The huge mass of the mountain, nearly twenty-five miles across at its base and towering over eleven thousand feet into the sky, seemed to fill the whole horizon, and Richter felt a deep sense of awe when he considered the vast natural forces that had created it. One day, he thought, as he automatically began his approach to land, man will learn to harness forces of that magnitude, and then he will either reach the stars or destroy himself.

Despite a fairly stiff crosswind—conditions under which the Messerschmitt 109F could be very tricky to land—all twenty-eight fighters got down without mishap. They taxied to their dispersals, waddling like ungainly birds as the pilots swung the long noses from side to side in order to see forward, using the throttle in short bursts and kicking up spurts of dust.

Richter shut down his engine, unlatched the cockpit hood and swung it over to the side. He unfastened his seat and parachute harness, stretched his arms high over his head with a grunt of relief, then levered himself upright from the narrow metal box of the cockpit, stepping out on to the wing. The heat of the sun was like a physical blow.

A corporal came running up, saluted, and informed him that transport would soon be arriving to take the pilots to their respective messes, a cluster of marquees on the far side of the airfield. Richter nodded, jumped down from the wing and wandered over to join Second Lieutenant Hans Weber, who was already stretched out on some sandbags. Richter grinned. Young Hans had arrived in Russia the previous November, straight from operational training school and green as grass. Richter had taken him under his wing, and Weber had flown as his number two ever since. He had fifteen Russians to his credit, and had already shown himself to be a fighter pilot of exceptional calibre. Richter wondered how the boy would shape up against the Tommies, who were a much tougher proposition than the Soviets. It would be an interesting exercise.

Richter punched the recumbent pilot lightly in the midriff. Weber opened one eye and grinned.

'Got any cigarettes?' Richter asked.

Weber sat up, fished in a pocket of his flying overall and brought out a crumpled packet. They both lit up, inhaling the smoke deeply.

'It's like a rest camp, this is,' Weber commented, looking about him. 'No more lice and stinking Ivans, no more worrying about partisans taking a pot-shot at you. Just look at it—beautiful sunshine, wonderful scenery, all that lovely warm sea, gorgeous dark-haired Sicilian maidens—why, it makes my balls ache just to think about it.'

Richter looked at him patronizingly, although he was only a couple of years older than Weber.

'You won't have any balls left unless you listen to my advice,' he said darkly. 'You have yet to meet your first Tommies. They aren't like the Ivans, you know. They can fly, make no mistake about that, and fight too. It's a pretty unnerving experience, that first time you find a Spitfire on your tail.'

'Well,' said Weber, grinning hugely, 'you managed to survive, so I reckon I stand an even better chance.'

Richter took a playful swipe at him. 'Why, you cheeky young puppy,' he laughed, 'I've a good mind to—'

The roar of massed aero-engines interrupted his words, a distant sound as yet, but growing louder with every second. Both men turned their heads, peering into the southern sky, and immediately picked out a cluster of aircraft, heading towards the airfield at a fairly low altitude. Even at this range, they were easily identifiable as Junkers 87 Stukas.

The Stukas arrived overhead and went into line astern,

circling the field. All except one. Trailing a thin ribbon of smoke, it came straight in to land, touching down heavily and bouncing a couple of times before rolling unsteadily across the field and stopping, its engine still turning. An ambulance and fire tender raced to meet it. Men jumped on to the Stuka's wing, slid back the perspex hoods that covered the pilot's cockpit and rear gunner's position. Richter and Weber watched, shading their eyes against the fierce glare of the sun, as the two crew members were helped from the aircraft and into the waiting ambulance. The pilot seemed to be all right, but the gunner had to be carried.

The other Stukas landed, in pairs, and taxied over to the far side of the field. Gazing around, Richter noticed that Catania housed a considerable collection of aircraft. As well as the newly-arrived Messerschmitts of Fighter Wing 66, and the Stukas, he recognized Junkers 88s, a small number of three-engined Junkers 52 transports, Italian Macchi 202s and Reggianes, and a few more Italian types he was unable to identify. All of them were well dispersed around the field.

'Looks like our transport,' Weber remarked.

A five-ton Italian Fiat truck, snub-nosed and distinctive, was bumping towards them around the perimeter of the field. A second vehicle followed, some distance behind. Richter stubbed out his cigarette, then turned to have a brief word with the mechanics who were carrying out the post-flight inspection of his Messerschmitt. By the time he had finished, the trucks had arrived and the pilots were climbing aboard.

Richter threw his parachute and lifejacket into one of the vehicles, clambered up over the tailboard and sat down on one of the hard benches that ran the length of the truck. As the Fiat moved off, he surveyed the faces of the other pilots, faces that had become so familiar to him since he had taken over command of Fighter Wing 66's 2nd Squadron last January.

There was little Johnny Schumacher, smoking his pipe imperturbably as usual, lost in his private thoughts. Warrant Officer Kurt Buchada, one-time boxing champion with his squashed, friendly face. Lieutenant Ernst Sommer, quiet and withdrawn except when he was drunk, when he could unearth a fund of riotous stories. Big, blond Willi Christiansen, whose father was a Norwegian and who spent all his leaves fishing, usually miles away from anywhere. Jürgen Baars, the squadron clown and the devil incarnate when it came to either women or fighting—usually a combination of both. Hans Weber . . . Johann Ruge . . . and the others, first-rate types all of them, forming a fighting unit with a proud record.

Richter felt a sudden twinge of sadness. He had seen so many of his friends die, had come close to death himself on more than one occasion, in the embattled skies from England to the Ukraine. Franz Peters, cut off by Hurricanes from the rest of his squadron, the remains of his body scattered over the chalky soil of Kent . . . Sergeant Dieter Brandtner, swallowed up by the English Channel . . . even Colonel Becker, the old invincible at whose side Richter had flown and fought almost from the very beginning, lost without trace somewhere over the icy steppes.

Although he tried his best to push such thoughts from his mind, he found himself wondering how many of the boys seated around him now would still be here in six months, or even a month. The thought never entered his head that one day, one of the empty places at the messroom dining-table might be his own.

Later, after an excellent meal prepared by Italian cooks and washed down with liberal quantities of Marsala wine, the newly-arrived pilots, fed and rested, assembled in the open air under the shade of an awning to be briefed by the base commander at Catania, Colonel Anton Dessauer. A small, wiry man, Dessauer was one of the Luftwaffe's leading dive-bomber pilots. He wore the Knight's Cross, chain-smoked cheroots and was a minor volcano of nervous energy.

He delivered a hasty welcoming address, then got down to the main business without further preamble. Lighting another cheroot, he surveyed the pilots for a few seconds, as though seeking the best choice of words, then said: 'Gentlemen, let me explain to you why you are here. Doubtless you have wondered why, at the height of the summer offensive in Russia, you were suddenly uprooted and sent to Sicily, when many of the air units which sustained the air offensive against Malta over the past few months have been transferred to the theatre you have just left.'

Richter thought that Dessauer looked slightly bitter, and knew the reason. By all accounts, the Luftwaffe units had been having a tough time in the Malta battle, and now several of the most experienced fighter and bomber groups had been stripped from II Air Corps just when the battle appeared to be on the point of being won.

'I have to tell you,' Dessauer went on, 'that events in the Mediterranean Theatre have suddenly taken a new turn. At noon yesterday, 26 May, General Rommel's Panzer Army Africa launched a new offensive against the British line at Gazala. The attack appears to be going well, and if it continues to do so we hope that our forces will be in Egypt inside a month. All this means that Malta has assumed a fresh priority, for we may assume that the British will once again use the island as a base for further attacks on our supply lines across the Mediterranean.'

Dessauer paused, flicked his half-smoked cheroot into the dust and passed a hand over his face, dislodging several flies. 'We chased them away, gentlemen,' he continued. 'Oh, yes, we chased away their bombers and their destroyers and their submarines and flattened their bases, but now they'll be back and we shall have to chase them away all over again, although this time with far fewer aircraft, which means that we shall have to fly and fight twice as hard as before. You, the fighters, must establish total air superiority over the island. The British will doubtless attempt to fly in more Spitfires very soon; you must destroy them on the ground. You must keep up the pressure relentlessly, day after day. Remember: you are just as much part of General Rommel's great offensive as if you were providing air cover for his tanks.'

Richter was beginning to feel bored. More than that: he felt disappointed. Dessauer had, at first, given the impression of a man who would present the facts, all of them, with no embellishment, and now here he was, delivering an address which was rapidly becoming the sort of thing a Party propagandist would try to put over.

He looked around covertly at the faces of the other pilots. Some of them, the younger ones, were leaning forward on their seats, listening intently as the colonel droned on, but most, the old hands, wore expressions ranging from dull resignation to acute exasperation. They had heard it all before.

There was no flying for the new arrivals that afternoon, two groups of Fighter Wing 53 at Gerbini having been detailed to carry out bomber escort duties and offensive patrols, so the pilots, whooping like savages and in high spirits, commandeered whatever transport they could find and headed for the town of Catania. Only Johnny Schumacher and Richter stayed behind, the former to write letters and the latter to familiarize himself with the airfield and its other occupants.

Determined to find out what conditions over Malta were really like, he borrowed a motor cycle and set off across the airfield towards the Stuka squadron, whose readiness tents were pitched in the shade of a clump of gnarled trees.

Ground crews were working on the dive-bombers, one or two of which showed signs of battle damage. Richter dismounted and strolled over to one of the aircraft and inspected its fin and rudder, which had been peppered by shell fragments. As he walked round the rear fuselage, a corporal in oil-stained overalls approached him and came to attention, saluting.

'Good afternoon, Herr Hauptmann,' he said respectfully, his eyes taking in Richter's decorations. 'May I be of assistance?'

'Are any of your officers here?' the pilot asked.

'I beg to inform the captain,' the man replied, using the formal style of address, 'that the squadron has been stood down for the afternoon and that only the duty officer is here.

He is in the operations caravan. If the captain will be kind enough to accompany me—'

Richter waved a hand, interrupting him. 'No, please don't bother,' he said. 'Carry on with the good work. I'll find the duty officer myself.'

The caravan stood at the far end of the flight line, beyond the cluster of tents, half hidden among the trees. The duty officer, a ginger-haired first lieutenant, sat on the steps, reading a magazine. He looked up, startled, as Richter's shadow fell over him, then jumped to his feet.

'My apologies, Herr Hauptmann,' he began. 'I didn't see you coming. I was just—'

He broke off suddenly and looked in puzzlement at Richter, whose face was split by a broad grin.

'Hello, Conrad,' Richter said.

The other's face cleared at once and he let out a yell.

'Jo Richter! Christ, man, I don't believe it! It's been years!'

He grabbed Richter in a bear hug, then held the laughing pilot at arm's length. 'Well, I'm damned,' he exclaimed. 'I can't get over this. I was just talking about you the other day. About that time you and I and Franz Bauer came across that "Strength Through Joy" camp when we were on manoeuvres. All those beautiful blonde Hitler maidens, just dying to give it away to the Führer's gallant soldiers! God, we were worn out for a fortnight!'

'We were bloody lucky we didn't get caught,' Richter laughed. He felt his spirits uplifted tremendously. It was good to see Conrad Seliger again. The two had gone through all their training together right up to operational training stage, when Richter had been posted to fighters and Seliger to bombers, much to his disgust. After that they had lost touch completely, although their minds held memories of a host of shared experiences, both good and bad.

Seliger led his friend into the caravan, which was furnished with a trestle table, a radio set, a field telephone and a couple of wickerwork chairs. Richter stretched out in one of them while Seliger rummaged in a map locker, unearthing a half-empty bottle of schnapps and a pair of tin mugs.

'It's not much,' he said, waving a hand at their surroundings, 'but it's home, at least for today. There's nothing going on this afternoon, as far as we are concerned, so it's nice and quiet.'

He filled the mugs, and they drank to old times, reminiscing over mutual escapades. At length, Richter said:

'It's a pity Franz Bauer isn't with us. The old team would be complete, then.'

A shadow crossed Seliger's face, momentarily.

'Franz is dead,' he said quietly. 'He didn't make it through the OTU. We were on dive-bombing practice one morning; he was ahead of me in the dive and I saw his tail come off. He went straight in. Nothing left.'

Richter was silent for a few moments. Then he raised his mug and said: 'Well, here's to Bauer.'

They drank. Richter looked at Seliger and changed the subject.

'Were you on the raid this morning?'

Seliger shook his head. 'No, I was on duty here. In any case, my aircraft was unserviceable. The boys didn't have too much trouble, though. One crew wounded, but they brought their Stuka back. They'll recover.'

Richter raised an eyebrow. 'Not too much trouble? It didn't look that way to me, judging by the number of holes in your crates.'

Seliger laughed. 'Oh, I assure you, Jo, this morning's raid was a milk run, compared to most. We were in and out before they knew what was happening.'

Richter set aside his mug and leaned forward, looking his friend directly in the eyes.

'Look, Conrad,' he said, 'what's it really like over there? Come on now, straight from the horse's mouth. No bullshit. According to Colonel Dessauer, we're walking all over the Tommies.'

Seliger's lip curled. 'Oh, him,' he said contemptuously. 'He's been giving you one of his celebrated pep talks, has he? Well, you don't want to take any bloody notice of what he says. All right, so he's had a distinguished career. I don't deny that, and that's why he was sent here in the first place, to bolster our morale. I don't mind admitting, Jo, our morale was pretty bloody low at one point, in March this year. We'd been taking losses. In fact, we're taking losses all the time. Dessauer doesn't know the half of it, because he's never been over there. It's not really his fault; higher authority reckons he's too valuable to risk his neck.'

He paused, and poured a little more schnapps into their mugs. Somewhere across the airfield, an engine coughed into life and roared healthily for a few moments before its note died away to a low rumble.

'Go on, Conrad,' Richter urged. 'Let's have the full story.'

'That I can give you,' Seliger said, 'because I first came here in April '41, during the first offensive against Malta. Now, I'd survived the big daylight attacks on England the year before, and I thought I knew all there was to know about flak—but I'm telling you, the flak over Malta, and especially Valletta, has to be seen to be believed. You can practically walk on it. Their barrage is centrally controlled, and you've got layers of flak plastering the sky at varying heights between fifteen hundred and four thousand metres over the target. Even if you manage to get through that lot, light flak in and around the objective can give you an awful lot of trouble. I'm glad I'm flying Ju 87s; at least we are pretty manoeuvrable and can avoid a lot of the muck by rapid course-changes. The Ju 88s are not so fortunate, and we've lost a lot to flak. The Italians are the luckiest, because they almost always go in at high level, where they have only the fighters to contend with.'

'Ah yes, the fighters,' Richter interrupted. 'From the way you talk, I get the impression that they rate a poor second to the flak.'

The other shook his head. 'No,' he said, 'I didn't mean to imply that at all. They didn't give us too much trouble during the first offensive, because the Tommies only had a handful

91

of Hurricanes and our fighter escort managed to keep them pinned down. They were still using Hurricanes in December, when I came back to Sicily after six months in the Balkans, and we still had the upper edge—in fact even more so, because the fighter boys were now flying Messerschmitt 109Fs and the Tommies were no match for them.'

Seliger took another swallow of the fiery spirit, pulled a long cigar from his shirt pocket and lit it carefully. Addressing Richter through a cloud of blue smoke, he went on:

'It was in April, about the middle of the month I think, when we got our first nasty shock. We hadn't encountered any fighter opposition for days and we'd dropped so many bombs on Malta that the place looked like the surface of the moon. We certainly hadn't counted on meeting Spitfires, but they were there all right. We lost a lot of aeroplanes that day. The Tommies brought in more Spitfires later in the month, and another batch about three weeks ago. It's no picnic any more.'

'Where the blazes do they come from?' Richter wanted to know. 'The Spitfires, I mean.'

'They fly 'em off carriers, apparently, well outside our range. It's a hell of a long haul for the pilots, but we hit the carriers pretty hard last year and the Tommies don't like to risk them any more. It makes things very hard for the convoys they are trying to push through to Malta—we really plaster them, and hardly any of the ships get through. I expect that when the island has run out of essential supplies such as fuel, and the population is starving to death, we'll walk in and take over.'

'Do you think there'll be an invasion soon?' Richter asked him. Seliger shrugged.

'Who can say?' he answered. 'All I know is that there are a lot of paratroops in southern Italy, and I've seen gliders in crates tucked away on airfields right here in Sicily, all ready to be assembled. I don't know why the hell we didn't invade the place months ago, before the Tommies had a chance to get organized.'

'Too busy in the Balkans and Russia, I suppose,' Richter

said. 'I must admit, though, I've often wondered why we didn't give more priority to Malta. It seems senseless to let Rommel go dashing off to Cairo with a British base in his rear, threatening his lines of communication.'

'It was senseless to attack Russia, too,' grunted Seliger. 'but we still did it. Well, now it's your turn to tell me something of what things are like there. The way I ramble on, I'm bound to upset somebody sooner or later and get myself sent to the Russian front. I might as well be prepared.'

They sat and talked together for the remainder of the afternoon, and Richter could not remember a time when he had enjoyed himself so much in the last couple of years. From time to time their conversation was interrupted by the shrill clamour of the telephone, or by the entry of engineer officers or NCOs who wanted to get in touch with some other section on the airfield. One or two pilots drifted in, stayed for a while and chatted politely with Richter, then wandered off to have a word with the men who were servicing their aircraft.

Only when they were alone did they speak of the conduct of the war, and the future of Germany, and only then because they trusted one another implicitly. Richter had seen men disappear overnight, quietly and with few questions asked, because their conversation in the Mess or the crew-room had implied criticism of the way the Nazis were running things. The regulations on 'defeatist talk', Richter had noticed, had been tightened up considerably since the German offensive in Russia had ground to a halt at the end of 1941.

Quietly, Richter discussed the things he had seen and heard with Seliger, and in the end came to the conclusion that such procedures were probably a necessary evil in time of war. Nevertheless, there were rumours, ugly whispers of the fate that befell those who opposed the aims of the Nazis, even in a minor way. Johnny Schumacher, returning from leave, had spoken of a party he had attended in Berlin. He had overheard snatches of conversation from a group of SS officers, all of them drunk: talk of executions and beatings, of men and women stripped naked and made to run round the compound of some camp in the middle of winter until they dropped from exhaustion and froze to death where they had fallen. The ss men had laughed until the tears rolled down their cheeks, it was such a huge joke. Johnny Schumacher could not remember the name of the camp; he thought it was somewhere in Poland.

Richter had not believed half the story. The ss were braggarts, Hitler's nancy-boys, treating the rest of the Wehrmacht with contempt. Richter was certain that the Wehrmacht would stand up to them in the long run, and that there would be a big sorting-out after the war was won. He voiced his opinion to Seliger, who nodded in full agreement.

The thought that Germany might lose the war did not even cross the mind of either man. It was the summer of 1942, and the eagles of the Third Reich were still soaring high.

Chapter Seven

Tony's bar in Sliema was crammed with every conceivable kind of uniform. Yeoman and Powell had found themselves a table in one corner, and now they were surveying the scene through an alcoholic haze. Their forty-eight-hour pass would soon expire and they were morose, a condition aggravated by the amount of whisky and gin inside them.

Yeoman stared into the bottom of his glass, reflecting on the events of the last couple of days. He summed them up in four words.

'Waste of bloody time.'

Powell looked at him. 'What is?' he asked.

Yeoman waved an unsteady hand. 'This lot. Our leave. Everything. Bombed to hell half the time, the hotel where we should have stayed in Valletta knocked flat. Should have stayed in Naxxar. Bloody waste of time.'

'Well,' Powell said truculently, 'whose fault's that? What about those two chicks we picked up in the Union Club, those telephonists? With their own apartment, and all? A real exhibition you made of yourself, and no mistake, with that brunette. Pouring gin down her cleavage just because she upset you!'

'She was a silly bitch,' Yeoman grunted. 'It was just the way she went on. Nose in the air all the time, babbling on about the Navy. Wanted to take her down a peg or two, that's all.'

'You did that all right,' Powell admitted. 'I thought she

95

was going to take you apart. The thin veneer of civilization fell right off her, I can't deny it. But I was getting on famously with her mate, you sod! End of a beautiful dream, that was. Anyone would think you have something against women, permanently.'

Yeoman toyed with his glass. 'Maybe I have, at that,' he said quietly.

Powell looked at him sharply, sensing that there was something more deeply ingrained in Yeoman's character than he had imagined.

'All right,' he said, 'you can tell your Uncle Gerry. You got a girl back home?'

Yeoman was silent for a few moments, lost in thought. Then he said:

'I thought I had. Someone I met when I was in France. She was an American—a newspaper correspondent.'

He lapsed into silence, remembering. Julia Connors. Julia of the red hair and the green eyes, who had told him that she loved him. The memory of the smooth touch of her skin was almost more than he could bear.

'Well, what happened?' Powell asked impatiently.

Yeoman sighed. 'We saw each other in London a few times after that,' he said, 'then she was recalled to New York. She promised she'd write, but she never did—or at least I never received any letter. I made some enquiries and learned she'd been sent to Burma to report on the American Volunteer Group.'

'So she'd still be there when the Japs attacked?'

'I hope not, but I'm very much afraid you're right. Anyway, there's damn all I can do about it. The trouble is, I can't get her out of my system, not even when I'm with some other woman. I just have this strong feeling I'm going to see her again and I want it all to be right with us, like it was before.'

'This war's a bastard,' Powell said sympathetically. 'Tough luck, old son. It'll probably all work out in the long run.'

Yeoman drained his glass, grimacing as the neat spirit hit his throat.

'It's nobody's problem but mine,' he said. 'It would just help if I knew she was okay, that's all. Anyway, let's change the subject. I feel depressed enough as it is.'

'Me too,' Powell agreed. They looked round; the noise in the bar was frightful and images were blurred through drifting tobacco smoke.

Yeoman's eyes focused on a group of Merchant Navy officers, standing in the far corner. He wondered where they had come from, as no vessels had got through to the island for some time, then realized that they must be the survivors of previous convoys whose ships had been sunk during the unloading process. He thought about going over and having a word with them, then dismissed the idea. They seemed quite happy on their own, and anyway he was not really in a conversational mood.

He looked at his watch. It was a little after half-past nine. Abruptly, he turned to his friend.

'What say we get out of this dump?' he queried. Powell shrugged.

'If you like,' he said. 'What's the suggestion—back to Valletta?'

Yeoman shook his head. 'No, I was thinking about going back to Naxxar. I don't know about you, but I've had enough of this.'

Powell looked startled. 'Back to Naxxar? How the hell are we going to get there at this time of night?'

'We'll walk,' Yeoman said. 'It's a nice night and I could do with some fresh air. A lot of it, in fact.'

Powell groaned. 'You're bloody well mad,' he said. 'Still, if you're determined to shove off, I'm not staying around here on my own. Come on, we might as well grab our gear.'

They went upstairs to the room they had rented above the bar and collected their bags. Yeoman left a couple of pounds on the table and they slipped quietly out of the building, not wishing to be waylaid by the friendly proprietor.

Outside they paused, sniffing the night air. Sliema Bay lay

directly in front of them, its placid water reflecting the light of the stars. Behind them, past the buildings of the town, the velvet of the sky gave way to a more luminous, lighter blue where the upper atmosphere caught the last flicker of the day from far beyond the curve of the earth.

'What's the quickest way?' Powell asked.

Yeoman frowned, considering the question, then said: 'Well, we can go down through Floriana and Birkirkara, the way we came, but it might be quicker to go straight through the town towards St. Julian's and then turn off.'

'Might get lost, that way,' observed Powell.

'Some bloody navigator you'd make,' Yeoman said. 'We've got the stars for reference, haven't we? Come on, let's go up through the town.'

They set off, keeping to a westerly course as far as the windings of the narrow streets would permit. Maltese men, seated in their open doorways and smoking pungent tobacco, called out greetings to them as they passed. Children, elfin-like in the shadows, darted to and fro across their path; many Maltese families had a habit of allowing their children to stay up until they became sleepy, which to Yeoman seemed far more sensible than the traditional English fashion of packing them off to bed at seven o'clock. Then he remembered that Maltese children usually slept for a couple of hours in the afternoon, which presumably meant that they had a lot of surplus energy to dissipate later on.

There were not many servicemen here, away from the waterfront bars; in fact Yeoman and Powell had walked on for a good ten minutes without seeing a uniform, so it came as something of a surprise when they suddenly heard the sound of loud voices, singing an unmistakably English song:

'Oh, we're off to see the Wild West Show,

The elephant and the kangaroo-oo-oo,

Never mind the weather, as long as we're together

We're off to see the Wild West Show!'

Four men burst out of a side street, almost running full tilt into the RAF officers. They wore naval uniforms, and one of them let out a yell:

'Hey, Air Force! Come on, we're all off to the party.'

'As a matter of fact,' said Yeoman, heartily wishing he had taken refuge in the shadows, 'we were just on our way—'

'No excuses, now!' cried the naval lieutenant, for such the rank badges on his epaulettes proclaimed him to be. 'Come on, chaps—press gang!'

Two laughing, cheering naval officers seized Yeoman by the arms and propelled him along the street, while Powell was kidnapped in similar fashion. After a few yards, Yeoman gave in and surrendered with as much grace as he could muster.

'All right,' he said, 'what's all this about a party?'

'Naval secret,' the lieutenant grinned. 'You'll find out, soon enough. Not far to go now.'

'Where are you from?' one of the other officers wanted to know. 'Takali?'

'No, Luqa,' Yeoman told him. 'What about you?'

'Hal Far. We're Fleet Air Arm, for the benefit of you ignoramuses.'

'Ignorami,' Yeoman solemnly corrected him. 'Are you fighter boys?'

'Well, sort of,' the other said. 'We've got three Hurricanes between us, but we sling a couple of 250-pounders under 'em and make fast attacks on targets in Sicily. We really stirred the wops up at Syracuse the other day—we knocked out half a dozen flying-boats and then broke all records for low-level flying on the way back.'

'It's nice to know we're hitting back,' Yeoman commented. 'See if you can clobber a few Stukas, while you're at it.'

'No bloody fear, old boy. That's your job. Too much flak around their airfields, all of it nasty.'

Yeoman suddenly remembered Russell Kemp, the young naval pilot who had served with him at Tobruk and in Crete the year before, and asked if anyone knew him. The question was answered by one of the men walking with Gerry Powell, a couple of steps behind, his accent betraying the fact that he was a Scot.

'Why yes, I do, quite well as a matter of fact.' There was a note of surprise in his voice. 'We trained together, and we've been bumping into each other at intervals for ages. Let's see —I last saw Russ Kemp in December, I think it was. He was on his way to join *Victorious*, escorting convoys to Russia, or something. How do you happen to know him?'

Briefly, Yeoman related the story of their adventures, of the hopeless last battle in Crete with a handful of worn-out fighters. Just as he was finishing, the little group reached what was clearly its destination, a large flatroofed house set back some distance from the road. Yeoman suddenly became aware that they had been climbing steadily as they walked. The house stood at the top of a rise, commanding an excellent view of the lower part of Sliema and the sea beyond. Although it was hard to tell in the darkness, it seemed to have been untouched by the bombing that had laid waste large tracts of the town.

They passed through a courtyard and stopped in front of an iron-bound wooden door. The house was blacked out, but the noise coming from inside confirmed that revelry of some sort was in progress.

The lieutenant groped for the bell-pull, found it and tugged. A minute later the door creaked open, and a man's voice said out of the darkness:

'Oh, hello, chaps. Do come in, but watch your step. Can't see a perishing thing.'

They went inside, stepping carefully over the threshold and the heavy door swung shut behind them. A moment later a match flared, and three candle flames grew, spreading their soft light over a large hallway.

The man who had admitted them, and who now held the candelabrum, was an army major. 'Sorry about this, chaps,' he apologized, 'but the wretched electricity went off twenty minutes ago. It's a good thing that Lucia's old man had the foresight to lay in a reasonable stock of candles. Come on, this way.'

Yeoman and Powell dumped their bags in the hall and followed the major and the Fleet Air Arm officers along a short corridor. The sound of music and voices swelled as they approached the door at the far end. The major flung it open with a cry of 'Reinforcements!' and they passed into the room beyond.

It was filled with the light of dozens of candles, their mellow glow softening the faces that turned towards the newcomers. Yeoman saw at a glance that the room was exquisitely furnished; he was seized by the strangest feeling of having been swept back in time, to an age of gentility that had no place under a rain of bombs.

The strains of Glen Miller's orchestra brought him back to reality, as someone put on another record, and he surveyed the people in the room. Many of the men—and some of the women, too—were in uniform, but there was a fair proportion of civilians. The naval officers appeared to be well known, for they dived into the throng and began talking to the other guests.

Yeoman saw that the lieutenant had seized a girl around the waist and was endeavouring to land a kiss on her cheek. Laughing, she was pushing him away. Yeoman looked away, then looked back with sudden interest, for the girl was beautiful—more beautiful than he had imagined at first glance.

'I'm for a basinful of that,' Powell murmured in his ear.

'Join the queue, you randy sod,' Yeoman told him. 'She's obviously too refined for the likes of you.'

The girl was petite, with grey eyes and blonde hair, but short. Her white dress clung to her shapely figure; the dress was sleeveless, revealing beautifully moulded arms.

She turned suddenly from the lieutenant and stared directly at Yeoman, who blushed despite himself, conscious that he had been undressing her mentally. She smiled and her face lit up, her eyes dancing. She said something to the lieutenant, who was whispering things in her ear. Rather reluctantly, he broke off and led her over to where the two RAF officers were standing.

101

'I say, chaps, sorry and all that, but I don't know your names,' he said uncomfortably.

Yeoman smiled, still blushing, and managed a small bow. He extended his hand to the girl.

'George Yeoman,' he said. 'And this is Flying Officer Gerry Powell.'

Her hand was cool and soft. A kind of electric shock spread up his arm. He was suddenly stone cold sober, and his tiredness and earlier despondency fell away as though someone had waved a magic wand.

'My name is Lucia Manduca,' she said softly. 'I am so pleased you could come.' She addressed the naval lieutenant. 'Peter, would you be kind enough to get your friends a drink?'

'Why yes, of course,' the lieutenant stammered. 'Whisky all right?'

'All right by me,' Yeoman said. 'Me, too,' Powell added. 'Thanks.'

Lucia turned back to face Yeoman. She reached out and touched him lightly on the arm.

'I hope you will enjoy yourselves,' she said. 'Please make yourselves completely at home. Now, if you will excuse me, I must attend to the rest of my guests. I will look forward to seeing you later.'

She smiled again, that utterly charming smile, and turned away, disappearing into the throng in a flurry of white, leaving a trace of perfume behind. In a kind of daze, Yeoman watched her go.

A glass was being pushed into his hand. Startled, he looked round to find the Army major grinning at him.

'So,' he said, 'I see that little Lucia has snared you in her tender web, too.'

'She's certainly fascinating,' Yeoman admitted. 'I'm puzzled, though. Is she Maltese? She speaks better English than I do.'

'As Maltese as they come,' the major assured him. 'She comes from a very old family—pretty high up among the

102

nobility in the old days, apparently. She was educated in England, of course.'

'And she lives here all by herself?' Yeoman wanted to know.

The major grinned and wagged a finger. 'Ah, now you're fishing, my boy. As a matter of fact, she doesn't. She has two sisters, both of whom are nurses, but they're on duty tonight. And there's her old man, of course, the baron.'

'Baron?' Yeoman said incredulously. 'You're kidding!'

'No, I'm not,' the major protested. 'He's a baron all right, although you wouldn't think it. He's a hell of a nice chap, very quiet and unassuming. He's on Gozo at the moment, has a villa there. Quite a distinguished war record in the last lot, I do believe. He's also a volunteer with the Royal Malta Artillery.'

'Well, I'll be damned!' Yeoman exclaimed. He thanked the major for the information, then moved off in search of Powell. The Canadian had knocked back three glasses of whisky so far and was engaged in a heated discussion with two Army types.

Yeoman left them to it and looked around for Lucia. She was seated on a triangular divan in one corner of the room, talking with an elderly, heavily bejewelled woman. Yeoman edged his way towards her, trying to appear nonchalant. She saw him coming out of the corner of her eye and looked up, smiling that terrific smile and beckoning to him.

He stood before her, feeling ridiculously self-conscious, as Lucia introduced him to the bejewelled lady, who inclined her head graciously as Yeoman took her hand. Privately, he was racking his brains in search of some way of getting Lucia alone for a few minutes. No one else in the room seemed to matter.

Lucia seemed to sense his discomfort. She shifted her place a little, then patted the divan to indicate that she wished the pilot to sit beside her. Yeoman did so, casting a sidelong glance at the elderly lady, who gave him a little smile and, so Yeoman swore later, what was almost a wink before turning away to speak to a young civilian who was standing nearby.

Yeoman cleared his throat and looked at Lucia, his stomach fluttering. Completely at a loss for any other comment, he said:

'I hear your father is a baron.'

Lucia's smile widened. She was obviously used to that particular opening remark. 'You hear correctly, Mr. Yeoman,' she told him. 'Are you familiar with our order of nobility?'

'Please call me George,' Yeoman said. 'No, I'm not, really. I suppose it has something to do with the Templars?'

She shook her head. 'Not at all. The Templars were never in Malta; that is a very popular misconception. The Knights of Malta were—and are—the Sovereign Military Order of St. John of Jerusalem, and the Maltese order of nobility existed for centuries before they came here. My father's family is descended from a knight, Simon de Molay, who helped Count Roger of Normandy drive the Moors from these islands in 1090. My mother came from an even older family, which was purely Maltese in origin; she was a Melac, and her ancestors were here long before even the Romans.'

Yeoman, vastly interested by all things historical, asked:

'Malta had a lot to do with Carthage then, hadn't it?'

Lucia nodded. 'Yes, Malta was a colony of the Phoenicians—who, of course, founded Carthage—for over a thousand years, and the language of Malta is Punic in origin, not a mixture of African and Sicilian. My mother's family name, Melac, had its origin in the Carthaginian cult of Moloch. It is probably one of the oldest surviving names in the world.'

She flashed her brilliant smile again. 'Did you know that there is considerable evidence that the tomb of the famous Hannibal lies somewhere on the edge of Hal Far airfield?' she asked.

Yeoman was forced to admit that he did not.

'Yes,' she continued, 'my father was trying to raise funds for an archeological dig when war broke out. He's a very keen amateur, you know, although a somewhat impecunious one. There are two classes of nobility in Malta, the rich and the poor, and I'm afraid Daddy belongs to the latter.

Anyway, he devotes most of his time to the Royal Malta Artillery now, and he seems to be very happy.'

'The RMA seems to be a very fine unit,' Yeoman commented. Lucia's eyes flashed with sudden pride.

'It is the only Maltese regular unit of the British Army,' she said. 'It was raised from the Cacciatori, the Irregulars, those of our people who rose against the French garrison of Napoleon and compelled it to surrender in 1800. In those days, there were—'

She stopped suddenly, halfway through the sentence. Conversation was stilled throughout the room as though a knife had sliced through it. The guests froze, listening, the flickering candle-flames throwing their shadows like grotesque statues on the delicate eggshell-blue colouring of the walls.

Far off, a siren had begun its unearthly wailing. It was taken up by others, the sound coming closer and closer until it made the night hideous.

'Oh, God,' Lucia said softly. Beside her, the elderly lady, swaying gently in her seat, her eyes closed, began to pray.

'Sliema Ghalik Marija . . . Missierna Li Inti Fis-Mewwiet . . .'

The major's voice sounded, breaking the tableau.

'All right, everybody, down to the cellar. Bring the candles with you. Last people out of the room, put out any candles that are left. Quickly, now! Let's hope the raid's a short one.'

Lucia suddenly placed her hand on Yeoman's arm. With a shock, he realized that she was trembling.

'Please,' she whispered, her voice small and frightened. 'I don't want to go down there. Not again. I can't stand being . . . below ground.' She was avoiding the words 'buried' or 'entombed'. 'Will you come up to the roof with me, out in the open?'

'It'll be dangerous,' Yeoman told her doubtfully. 'A lot of shrapnel comes down from the anti-aircraft barrage, and . . .'

'Please!' she said desperately, her eyes wide and marbled. His heart went out to her.

'All right,' he said gently, 'whatever you say.'

Gerry Powell appeared beside them. 'Come on, you two,' he said urgently. 'Let's get below decks.'

Yeoman shook his head. 'No, I'm going out on the roof with Lucia. We want to see what's going on.'

'Well,' said Powell, 'on your own heads be it. I'm off to play at being a rabbit. But watch yourselves, huh?'

He followed the other guests through the main door. Lucia took one of the candelabra and led Yeoman along a short corridor to the foot of a steep, winding staircase. They hurried up it, their footfalls sounding hollow and unreal, until they came to a small landing. There were doors on either side, presumably leading to attics, and one directly in front. Lucia extinguished the candles and opened it. They stepped out into warm night air.

'Be careful,' she whispered. 'Mind you don't trip. You had better take my hand.'

Yeoman lost no time in obeying. Together, they walked across the flat roof and stood by the railing that surrounded it.

The sirens had ceased their wailing and the night was completely still. The couple looked out over the darkened island, with its canopy of stars and the shimmering sea beneath. Not a glimmer of light was to be seen, not even a searchlight. There was no sound apart from a gentle sighing, coming from the sea.

'It's too quiet,' Yeoman said, his voice low. 'Unreal, almost.'

'Perhaps it was just a false alarm,' Lucia murmured hopefully.

'I doubt it,' Yeoman told her. 'They'll have picked up something definite on radar, and—'

He broke off as Lucia gripped his arm. 'Listen,' she said. 'I can hear them. They're coming.'

She was right. Far off in the darkness they could hear the steady drone of aero-engines, growing louder with every second. Yeoman turned his head from side to side, trying to locate the source of the sound, and a moment later his brow furrowed in perplexity. The swelling noise seemed to be coming from the south-east, the opposite direction to Sicily. Moreover, it bore little resemblance to the throbbing, de-synchronized note of the Junkers 88.

Suddenly, he knew it for what it was. In a surge of excitement, he put his arm around Lucia's shoulders and hugged her to him.

'They're ours,' he cried. 'The bombers are coming back —flying in from Egypt! It's all right, they're ours!'

Then another thought struck him. Why had the sirens sounded? Unless . . . unless the enemy knew about the incoming bombers and was sending in a raid to try and hit them as they landed.

He did not voice his thoughts to Lucia. Instead, he concentrated on the sound of the incoming aircraft, trying to work out how far away they were, praying that they all got down safely. The leading bombers, judging by their engine noise, were crossing the coast now, somewhere over towards Marsaxlokk. They seemed to be heading for Luqa. Yeoman tried to identify the signature of their engines: they didn't sound like Wellingtons. Probably Beaufort torpedo-bombers, he thought.

The note of the engines changed as the leading aircraft began its approach to Luqa, dying away to a dull rumble. Yeoman tried to count the bombers as they went in, his ears tuning to the sound of each one. He thought he counted six. They were all down. They had all made it.

Then the flashes burst across the skyline, throwing every-thing into stark relief for a second. The night closed in again, but not for long. In the direction of Luqa a dull red glow suffused the sky, and in that same instant they heard the crump of the explosions. They also heard the strident howl of more aero-engines, this time unmistakably German, accom-panied by the bark of cannon fire. Another fire flared, died briefly away and then flared more brightly close to the first, twin beacons in the darkness.

Belatedly the flak opened up, scattering pearls of light

across the sky over Luqa. Searchlights flicked on, their beams wavering uselessly across the sky, but the attackers had already gone.

'Someone's bought it,' Yeoman said dully, staring at the red glow. 'The Huns must have come in low, from the west, and jumped Dingli Cliffs. Sounded like Messerschmitt 110s.'

Beside him, Lucia shivered. His arm was still round her shoulders. 'Are you cold?' he asked.

'No. It's just that . . . I was thinking about those poor men in the bombers. Coming all this way, to help us, and then . . .'

He knew that she was weeping quietly, her tears hidden by the darkness, and held her closer to him.

'They didn't get them all,' he said lamely. 'Some of them got down all right.'

It was not over yet. Engines, many of them, drummed in the northern sky. The horizon twinkled with flashes as flak batteries opened up near Mellieha, the sound reaching Yeoman and Lucia seconds later, even before the shells exploded. The bombers were coming high, out of range of most of the anti-aircraft fire. They were probably Italian, although it was impossible to say with certainty.

The whole island seemed to shudder as the first sticks of bombs exploded somewhere near Takali. More bombs fell, creeping towards and across Luqa and Safi. It was as though the bombers were trying to break the spine of the island. The explosions formed a continuous drum-roll of noise, battering the senses.

'They're going for the airfields again,' Yeoman said. 'I think we're going to be all right, this time.'

The bombers were turning out to sea as soon as they released their loads, diving to pick up speed and endeavouring to keep clear of the mighty flak barrage around the Grand Harbour. Yeoman wondered why the Beaufighters had not taken off.

Not all the bombers succeeded in avoiding the barrage. Yeoman heard engines directly overhead, and a few moments later the night around their little rooftop island dissolved in

108

noise and lightning flashes as dozens of batteries opened up, spraying the sky with multi-coloured shell-bursts. Beneath their feet, the building trembled and vibrated violently.

There was a sudden rustling noise, a soughing of air nearby. Something struck the courtyard below with a clang. Instinctively, Yeoman moved closer to Lucia.

'That was shrapnel,' he said urgently. 'I suggest we move to a less exposed spot—the doorway, perhaps. We can watch from there, if you like.'

He led her, unprotesting, across the rooftop. In the open doorway they turned, standing close to one another, looking back at the savage firework display. The din was terrific, and Lucia pressed her hands to her ears. Yeoman pointed, mouthing words which she could not hear: high over Valletta the tiny moth-shape of a bomber was caught in a cone of searchlights, the sparks of the anti-aircraft shells dancing around it. It twisted and turned, spiralling down in its pool of vivid light, the glowing strings of shells creeping closer to it all the while.

Then suddenly it was gone, dissolving into a thousand incandescent embers that cascaded down through the night. Yeoman and Lucia watched them as they fell and were extinguished one by one. Only one large fragment still burned as it tumbled to earth, somewhere beyond Birkirkara.

Neither Yeoman nor Lucia said anything. There was nothing to say; what they had witnessed was remote and impersonal. Yeoman recalled, suddenly, how he had stood on the balcony outside the billet in Naxxar on his first night in Malta and witnessed the destruction of an enemy bomber, dwelling later in the silence of his room on the fate of its crew. Tonight, he felt no such sentiment, and did not know whether to be glad or sorry because of it.

The searchlights that had trapped the destroyed aircraft like a moth in a jar were now searching for other targets, but the bombers were departing, the sound of their engines fading away to the north-west. All except one.

Yeoman hurriedly pulled Lucia deeper into the shelter of the doorway as a faint whistling noise grew to a piercing shriek. The stick of bombs fluted overhead and the couple ducked as it exploded a few streets away with a massive crump that left their ears singing. In the wake of the explosions they heard the rumble of falling, sliding masonry.

'Probably a hung-up bomb load,' Yeoman said breathlessly. 'It's over now. They've gone.'

A few moments later the all-clear sounded. Lucia turned to Yeoman, looking up at him. Without warning, she stood on tiptoe and kissed him lightly on his cheek.

'Thank you,' she said simply. 'Thank you for taking care of me.'

Somewhat at a loss for words, Yeoman said: 'Well, we'd better go back inside. The others will be coming up from the shelter. They'll be wondering what happened to us.'

Yet neither of them made a move. Yeoman's brain was whirling, flashing with memories of another occasion, an age ago, when he had stood at a window in London and watched German bombs falling on the docks. Julia had been beside him, then.

But Julia was not here now, and Lucia was. Taking a deep breath, he blurted:

'Lucia—just before we go down, I'd like to ask you . . . I mean, may I come to see you again?'

She smiled, and squeezed his hand gently.

'I should like that,' she whispered. 'I should like that very much.'

Chapter Eight

The Luqa squadron was on dawn readiness, the Spitfires standing combat-ready in their blast pens, their pilots nearby. Yeoman leaned against the sandbags, idly watching the sunrise without really seeing it, turning over in his mind the words of the Air Officer Commanding Malta.

It was Monday, 15 June, and the AOC had addressed the pilots in Rabat the previous evening. His face had been grim, and he had not minced his words. There was a great deal of news, and all of it was bad.

Rommel had broken through at Gazala, mopping up large numbers of Commonwealth and Free French troops, destroying their supporting armour wholesale, his Panzers racing on towards Egypt and overrunning the Desert Air Force's forward airfields. Once again, the army was in full retreat, and the German success in North Africa meant that Malta's position was now more exposed than ever.

In an attempt to alleviate the island's desperate plight two convoys had been assembled: one at Alexandria and the other at Gibraltar. The latter, code-named 'Harpoon', had entered the Mediterranean during the night of 11 June; it consisted of six freighters strongly escorted by cruisers and destroyers and by the aircraft carriers *Eagle* and *Argus*. The other convoy, consisting of eleven freighters accompanied by seven cruisers and seventeen destroyers—almost the whole of the Mediterranean Fleet's effective strength—had sailed from

Haifa and Port Said two days later. It had no carriers, and consequently no air cover.

Starting at dawn on 13 June, the convoy from the east had come under savage air attack by Junkers 88 dive-bombers from Heraklion, in Crete, and before the day ended two freighters had been sunk and two more severely damaged.

That was bad enough, but there was worse to come. That same evening, Admiral Vian, commanding the naval escort, learned that units of the Italian Fleet—the battleships *Littorio* and *Vittorio Veneto,* together with four cruisers and twelve destroyers—had left the naval base at Taranto and were steaming south-eastwards. Knowing that he had little hope of defending the convoy in the face of such superior strength, particularly since the British ships were under constant and heavy air attack and were running short of ammunition, Vian at last decided to proceed no further and ordered the convoy to turn back to Alexandria. In addition to the merchant losses, the abortive operation had cost him a cruiser and three destroyers.

Everything now depended on the convoy from the west. On the thirteenth it was attacked sporadically by bombers from Sardinia and one ship was lost, but the following day it was attacked almost without pause by high-level and dive-bombers, and torpedo aircraft escorted by fighters. A handful of Sea Hurricane and Fairey Fulmar fighters from the two old carriers put up a spirited defence and managed to shoot down six Italian aircraft, but the aircraft carriers were scheduled to turn back after dark.

Yeoman squinted into the rising sun, wondering when they would receive the order to take off. Malta's three surviving Beaufighters had patrolled the convoy during the hours of darkness, as it slipped through the narrow channel between the coast of Tunis and the western tip of Sicily, but the really dangerous time began now, with the dawn, as the freighters —lightly escorted by a cruiser and five destroyers—entered 'Bomb Alley' on the final run to the beleaguered island.

Ten hours' steaming lay ahead of the convoy: a ten-hour nightmare through the most bitterly contested waters in the world, with the full weight of the Luftwaffe and the Regia Aeronautica in southern Itlay and Sicily devoted to its annihilation.

Sometime during the morning the convoy would reach a point seventy miles from Malta, when relays of Spitfires from Takali and Hal Far—every available aircraft—would endeavour to provide a continual air umbrella over the ships. Before that point was reached, however, there would be a critical forty-mile gap between first light and the maximum distance at which the Takali and Hal Far Spits could begin to provide cover.

That gap was to be filled by the Luqa Spitfires, fitted with long-range fuel tanks. Only Luqa had a long enough strip of runway to permit the heavily-laden fighters to take off. There were only twelve of them, and they would have to operate in sections of four: one section over the convoy, one on its way out and one on its way back.

Yeoman looked at his watch. Red Section, led by Roger Graham, had taken off twenty minutes earlier; any minute now it would be the turn of Yellow Section, led by himself. Gerry Powell was flying in the number two position, with Sergeant Wilcox and Pilot Officer Kearney, a burly Irishman, as Yellow Three and Yellow Four respectively.

Yeoman felt a shiver run along his spine and put it down to the aftermath of the Dog, an attack from which he had recently recovered. Gerry Powell had been right about the goat's milk, after all. Yeoman still felt washed out and in no fit state to lead four fighters into action against, possibly, twenty or thirty times their number.

This morning, coincidentally, Sykes and Tozer were once again his fitter and rigger, and for this Yeoman was glad; he enjoyed the cheerful banter of the two airmen. At Luqa, in these hectic days, it was rare to get the same ground crew twice; you grabbed whatever fighter was serviceable, and in the five weeks he had been on the island Yeoman had done the rounds of just about all the blast pens around the perimeter.

In his mind, he went over the latest situation reports.

113

While it was still dark, torpedo-carrying Beauforts had taken off to attack the Italian warships which, apparently, were still steaming in pursuit of the retreating Alexandria convoy; they had not yet returned. Those torpedo-bomber boys certainly earned their pay, he reflected, and recalled a conversation with one Beaufort pilot earlier that month. It wasn't so bad, the man had told him. Nothing could get at you on the way out to the target, or on the way home again; it was only over the target that all hell broke loose during the two or three minutes it took you to make your run and drop your torpedo, and if you got through that you were all right. Yeoman imagined flying straight and level into a solid wall of flak, a few feet above the waves, and shuddered. Anyway, the Beaufort pilot's luck had run out in the end. Only three days earlier, he had led a strike of four torpedo-bombers against an enemy convoy west of Pantellaria, and had flown into the side of an Italian freighter.

The Harpoon convoy was a long way behind schedule at the last report, with a hundred and forty miles still to run. By now, the enemy would be hurling everything at it.

Yeoman pushed himself away from the sandbags, startled by Tozer's sudden excited shout. The airman was pointing across the cratered field towards G Shelter, where a Very flare was tracing its smoky trail through the morning haze.

Sykes, the fitter, was already in the cockpit, and by the time Yeoman got there he already had the engine running. The airman relinquished his place and helped Yeoman to strap himself in, dropping off the wing as the pilot taxied forward and giving a thumb-up for good luck.

The other three Spitfires were emerging from their pens, dragging clouds of dust as they followed Yeoman to the runway. Since he was in the lead, he could afford the luxury of taking off with the cockpit hood open, gaining a few precious seconds of cooling breeze.

The Spitfire rumbled forward, swaying as he lined up with the centre of the runway and opened the throttle. The tail came up reluctantly as he eased the stick forward and the speed built up agonizingly slowly as the valiant Merlin

114

engine coped with the extra weight of the auxiliary fuel tank; he was almost despairing that the fighter would ever leave the ground when she bounced a couple of times and then wallowed into the air, the controls becoming more responsive as she gained flying speed steadily.

He pulled up the undercarriage and slammed the hood closed, turning quickly on to the heading that ought to bring them to the convoy, or what was left of it: 280 degrees magnetic. The other Spitfires slid into formation around him as he climbed, rocking their wings. Radio silence was to be maintained until they were over the convoy, or unless they ran into trouble en route; there was no point in advertising their movements to the enemy.

They flew on steadily for several minutes. Over on the left, a lump of rock emerged from the sea: the island of Linosa. Beyond it, there was nothing but a vast expanse of open sea.

It was as though the four Spitfires hung suspended in limitless space. There was no sense of movement; only the dials on the instrument panel betrayed the fact that they were cleaving through the air at two hundred and fifty miles an hour. After a while, Yeoman frowned and glanced at the chronometer. They had been airborne for thirty minutes, and by now they should be over the convoy. Yet there was nothing below them or anywhere in their vicinity, as far as they could see.

Yeoman decided that it was time to break radio silence and call up the destroyer which had been designated as control ship for the Malta-based fighters. He called several times, but there was no reply. The sudden, horrifying thought struck him that perhaps the fighter umbrella had come too late, and that the convoy had already been wiped out.

The radio crackled suddenly into life and Gerry Powell's voice sounded loudly in Yeoman's earphones.

'Yellow Two to Yellow One. There's a lot of smoke over on the horizon, at three o'clock.'

Yeoman peered over to the right, towards the narrow band of haze that lay between the horizon and the sky. A wide column of smoke was rising from it, like the peak of a mountain protruding through a layer of cloud.

'Okay,' Yeoman said. 'Let's go.' He swung his Spitfire round towards the north, followed by the others. If the smoke marked the position of the convoy, he thought, then it was a long way north of where it ought to be, dangerously close to the island of Pantellaria.

More smoke became visible as they flew on; great clouds of it, rolling across the sea. Suddenly, out of one of the clouds a ship emerged, her lines long and rakish, her upperworks gleaming white in the sun. Yeoman identified her as an Italian cruiser, and as he watched she loosed off a broadside towards some unseen target, her heavy-calibre guns belching sulphurous smoke across the sea. Another cruiser followed her, steaming in line astern, her outline trembling as she too fired a salvo.

The battle was not all one-sided. Near the rearmost of the cruisers, and just short of her, a line of waterspouts erupted and then collapsed slowly, leaving spreading circles of white foam on the surface of the sea. The warship began to turn away at speed, heeling over as she creamed through the waves.

Yeoman tensed involuntarily as anti-aircraft bursts peppered the sky some distance to the left. The leading cruiser had woken up to the fact that the four aircraft were enemies, and her superstructure twinkled with the flashes of her guns as she threw shells at them. The Spitfires swept through the drifting smoke of the bursts, which were creeping unpleasantly close; then the cruisers fell away astern and the fire died down.

The pilots could now see the source of the smoke which Powell had sighted initially. A large vessel lay listing and burning fiercely; because of the smoke and flames, which obscured her from stem to stern, it was impossible to tell whether she was a warship or a freighter. They circled her, alternately watching her end and keeping an eye on the sky.

In a sudden, horrific flash that was to remain imprinted on Yeoman's mind for a long time to come, she exploded. A great column of smoke and water and debris hurtled sky-ward, a visible shock wave rippling out around it. The column hung poised, then fell in on itself and cascaded back down to the surface. White splashes all around marked the spot where wreckage hit the sea. Then there was nothing but a great patch of oil, floating on the swell.

They cruised over the area, searching constantly. Large tracts of the sea were blanketed with a fog compounded of drifting smoke and haze, and it was difficult to penetrate it. They glimpsed several ships, mostly destroyers, but Yeoman was unable to tell whether they were friend or foe; they appeared to be steaming round in circles. One of them, which seemed to be British, opened up on the Spitfires as they sped past her; Yeoman could hardly blame the gunners for being trigger-happy after what they must have been through.

This was crazy; it was impossible to identify anything in all the chaos down below. All they were doing was cruising around helplessly, using up precious fuel. Their search had already consumed the best part of an hour, and their fuel state would soon become marginal. Yeoman led the Spitfires in one more sweep of the area, then made up his mind.

'All right, chaps, let's pack it in.' He made a rapid calculation. 'Course for home 068 magnetic.'

They turned towards the south-east, leaving the battle-torn patch of water behind them. Blue Section would soon be arriving to take over; Yeoman hoped they would have better luck.

'Yellow Four calling. Aircraft ten o'clock, low.' Yeoman turned his head as Kearney's Irish brogue sounded over the R/T. At first he failed to see them; Kearney must have excellent eyesight. Then, as his eyes focused, he picked out a flicker of movement low down against the sea, to the left of the Spitfire's nose.

'Roger, I have them.' He made a conscious effort to allow his eyes to relax, the surest way of sharpening one's vision slightly at long range. 'They look like biplanes.'

'They are biplanes!' Powell's voice broke in excitedly. 'Fiat CR 42s! Boy, we've got 'em all to ourselves!'

He was right. There were six of them, crawling slowly over the brilliant surface of the sea in arrowhead formation, following a south-westerly course.

'Hold it,' Yeoman warned. 'Wait till I give the word.' He made a careful scrutiny of the sky, above and behind and to either side; it was empty. The Fiats were abeam of them now, about three thousand feet low down.

Yeoman pressed the R/T button. 'Let's go,' he said laconically. 'Pick your own targets, but watch them—they're nippy.'

The Spitfires fanned out and went into a diving turn, curving down to get on the Fiats' tails. The Italian fighters maintained their impeccable formation and seemed to float towards the hurtling Spitfires like bumble-bees flying backwards. There was no mistaking the outlines of the stubby little radial-engined biplanes, with their upper wings much longer than the lower set, their fixed, spatted undercarriages and their open cockpits. Each of them carried an egg-shaped object slung under its fuselage between the undercarriage legs, but whether it was a bomb or an extra fuel tank it was impossible to tell at this distance.

The range narrowed steadily. The Spitfires, their reflector sights illuminated and their guns set to 'fire', were already only half a mile astern of the enemy fighters and closing fast.

Suddenly the enemy formation scattered in all directions, the leading pair of aircraft diving headlong towards the sea and those on either flank breaking wildly to left and right. Yeoman knew that the CR 42 was one of the few aircraft in the world that could out-turn a Spitfire, even though it was a good hundred miles an hour slower, and that if the Italian pilots had been a little quicker off the mark they could have used their manoeuvrability to good advantage, out-turning the Spits until the latter were forced to break off the action through lack of fuel.

Yeoman ignored the Fiats on the flank, catching a glimpse as they steep-turned past him in the opposite direction, shooting between them like a rocket and chasing the leading

118

pair, who had now levelled out a few feet above the sea. He made a rapid R/T call to Powell:

'Give the others a hand, Gerry. I'll handle these two.'

Powell acknowledged briefly, twisting away from his position a couple of hundred yards astern of Yeoman. A Fiat skidded across his nose and he fired, cursing as he saw his tracers go wildly astray.

Yeoman, meanwhile, was rapidly overhauling the two low-flying Fiats. The two black egg-shaped objects dropped away under them and splashed into the sea and an instant later the fighters split up, turning hard to left and right, their wingtips almost touching the water. Yeoman went after the Fiat on the left, cutting across its turn and firing as it crept into his sight. He saw his cannon shells churn up the sea, converging on the Fiat in a swathe of foam, and tensed ready to make a correction when the enemy fighter took evasive action. Instead it flew straight on, directly into the stream of shells, and came apart like matchwood. Its port wings ripped away completely, taking away with them part of the tail, and the remainder of the aircraft flicked into a series of rapid rolls before smacking into the water.

Yeoman flashed over the tangled, sinking wreckage and pulled up in a steep climbing turn to the right, looking for the other Fiat. He located it almost immediately, low over the water and heading flat out towards Sicily, and raced in pursuit. The enemy pilot saw him coming and entered a beautifully executed series of evasive manoeuvres, handling his fighter skilfully and edging closer to home all the time. Yeoman fired twice and missed, miscalculating the Fiat's speed badly and overshooting. The Italian disappeared under the Spitfire's port wing and Yeoman turned hard, looking down and behind. It was some moments before he sighted the Italian again; the enemy pilot had crossed under his turn, taking full advantage of the Spitfire's blind spot, and was once again making a beeline for the Sicilian coast.

Yeoman fired a last long burst in the direction of the fleeing fighter and then gave up the chase. His fuel was now dangerously low, and if he carried on the pursuit it was doubtful whether he would be able to reach Malta safely. Besides, he had a grudging admiration for the way the Italian had handled his outclassed biplane; he deserved to get away.

Yeoman turned on to a south-easterly heading and looked around. One by one, the other three Spitfires of his section converged on him. The battle had been short and one-sided; Yeoman's Fiat was the only one to succeed in getting away. Sergeant Wilcox, the Rhodesian, had shot down two, although not without some difficulty; he reported that one of the Italian fighters had managed to hit his Spitfire with an incredibly lucky deflection shot, but that everything seemed to be working all right. Powell and Kearney had got one apiece.

Together, the four Spitfires set course for home, nursing their precious reserves of fuel. They had the sky to themselves, and all seemed peaceful. Then, after ten minutes or so, Wilcox suddenly called up:

'Yellow Three to Yellow One. My engine temperature's rising badly. Will somebody give my Spit the onceover?'

There was a brief pause, and then Kearney said: 'It looks like you're losing glycol, Johnny. You're pulling a white trail. Not much, but visible.'

Wilcox's voice, in reply, sounded nervous. 'That bastard must have hit my coolant tank,' he said. 'Temperature's going off the clock now.'

Yeoman allowed his Spitfire to drop back until he was flying alongside Wilcox's aircraft. The trail of glycol was growing denser, and trickles of darker smoke were beginning to emerge from under the engine cowling.

'It doesn't look too good, Johnny,' he told the Rhodesian. 'Think you can make it?'

'I . . . I'm not sure. She sounds rough. Starting to vibrate a lot. I think I'd better get ready to ditch.'

'No, Johnny,' Yeoman said urgently. 'Don't try and ditch. I repeat, do not try to ditch.' The auxiliary fuel tank, which could not be jettisoned in flight, would be a dangerous obstacle in the way of an attempted landing on the sea, and might drag the Spitfire down like a stone.

120

'Why . . . oh, Roger. The tank. I'd forgotten . . . Okay, getting ready to bale out.'

Yeoman saw Wilcox slide back his cockpit hood and unfasten his seat harness. The smoke was getting worse, partly obscuring the cockpit and the hunched figure of the pilot.

'Try and stretch it as long as you can, Johnny,' he said. 'Another fifteen minutes will see us home.'

'Roger . . . I don't think she'll hold that long.' Wilcox's voice was growing more tense and strained as the seconds ticked away. 'She's shaking like hell.'

Yeoman made no reply. There was nothing to say. He was imagining the ordeal Wilcox was going through, because he himself had experienced something similar on more than one occasion. Sweat pouring into the eyes . . . hands slippery on the stick, the needles on the instruments coldly spelling out one's fate.

'She's gone.' The words were flat and without emotion. Wilcox's Spitfire began to go down, shrouded in smoke, its engine seized and useless.

'I'm getting out now. So long, chaps.'

The Spitfire rolled over on its back, and Yeoman saw the dark bundle of Wilcox's body drop from the cockpit, curving down toward the sea. Yeoman felt a flood of relief as the Rhodesian's parachute streamed and then deployed fully; at least he was safe so far.

Their low fuel state did not permit them to circle the spot until Wilcox climbed into his dinghy. All Yeoman could do was to put out a distress call to Malta's air-sea rescue service and hope for the best. He made up his mind that if he could secure permission, he would take off again as soon as possible and take part in the search.

The rest of the flight back to the island was without incident, the Spitfires landing at Luqa shortly after the returning Beaufort torpedo-bombers, or what was left of them. Two had been shot down, a third had crashed on landing and the others had been punched full of holes. Nevertheless, they brought back a report of success: their

121

torpedoes had hit two Italian cruisers and a destroyer. The Malta garrison would not know it for some time, but the Beauforts' gallant torpedo strike had so unnerved the Italian naval commander that he had turned his force round and headed back towards Taranto. The convoy from Alexandria would have been able to get through after all.

All four of Roger Graham's Spitfires had got back safely, and the squadron commander told Yeoman that they had arrived over the convoy just in time to break up an attack by a large formation of Stukas. The dive-bombers had been unescorted and the Spitfire pilots had destroyed five of them, Graham himself accounting for two, before shortage of fuel had forced them to break off the action.

Yeoman asked if he might go out again in search of Wilcox but Graham refused, pointing out quite rightly that fuel was desperately scarce and that there was none to spare for what might easily turn out to be a wild-goose chase. Fishing pilots out of the sea was the job of air-sea rescue, and they did it very efficiently. Besides, Wilcox had come down approximately in the path of the convoy, and there was a reasonable chance that a passing ship might pick him up.

But Wilcox never returned to Malta. A long time later, Yeoman learned that he had been rescued by an Italian flying-boat and flown to Syracuse. The Rhodesian was destined to spend the rest of the war as a prisoner.

The Luqa Spitfires, refuelled and re-armed, nestled in their pens while their pilots waited, sweltering in the heat, for orders to take off on a second mission to the convoy. Most of them remained in the vicinity of G Shelter, wandering down the steps from time to time to take advantage of the coolness and to hear the latest reports on the convoy's progress. A couple of tents had been rigged up nearby, the stone hut that had served as the mess having been flattened some time ago, but no one was using them; the heat inside, and the stuffiness, were unbearable.

Yeoman sat on the rocks outside the shelter, sharing a mug of tea with a flight lieutenant who had come down from Takali on some errand or other. The man looked utterly haggard, and Yeoman realized with a sudden shock that he must look much the same himself. They were all worn out, and for some the strain had become too much. The man who now sat next to Yeoman was showing all the classic symptoms of the Malta fighter pilot's 'twitch'. When he spoke, his voice was dull and monosyllabic.

'They shot a kid at Takali the other day,' he said suddenly.

'They did what?' Yeoman asked, startled by the other's comment.

'Shot a kid. At Takali. A young Malt.'

'What the hell for?' Yeoman wanted to know.

'They said it was sabotage. He was one of the kids who help out, refuelling the Spits and so on. You know.'

Yeoman nodded. Luqa, too, had its share of young Maltese, local boys who had volunteered to fetch and carry and generally do odd jobs around the airfield. They did their work proudly and extremely well, and the few shillings they earned was a welcome extra source of income for their families.

'He was only a kid,' the flight lieutenant went on, staring at the dusty ground between his feet. 'Couldn't have been more than seventeen. A hell of a nice lad. Got on well with everybody. The erks thought the world of him.'

'What did he do?' Yeoman asked.

'Poured some oil into a Spit's fuel tank,' the other replied. 'Everybody swore it was an accident, but it made no difference. You know the orders: anybody found guilty of sabotage or theft, whether he's service or civilian, is liable to be summarily tried and executed. So they shot the poor little bastard. In front of everybody.'

Yeoman was silent, thinking. Drastic measures were certainly necessary to preserve security and discipline in an island under siege, but surely . . . to shoot a mere boy for something he didn't intend seemed utterly heartless, calculated to inculcate hatred among the islanders. And yet, on the other side of the coin, the boy's action might have cost the life of a pilot, had the slip not been detected in time. It all took a lot of weighing up, but there was something barbaric

123

and horrible about putting someone before a firing squad —and a civilian, at that—with hundreds of personnel looking on.

'I'll bet they wouldn't have done it if it had been one of our blokes,' he commented.

His companion looked at him and nodded slowly. 'I'm inclined to agree with you,' he said. 'Wherever we go, the Brits I mean, we seem to take it out on the poor bloody natives.' He smiled thinly. 'Remember the old saying about the colonial British? "I can't understand why they don't like us," said the District Commissioner, idly flicking a passing wog with his bull whip!'

Yeoman grinned. 'There's a lot of truth in that,' he said. 'But I've a feeling there'll be big changes when all this lot is over. There won't be an Empire any more, at least not as we used to know it.'

He stood up, and the flight lieutenant looked at him quizzically. 'What are you,' he asked jokingly, 'some sort of bloody bolshevik?'

'No,' Yeoman smiled, 'just what you might call a realist. I'm off downstairs to see what's going on. Coming?'

The other shook his head. 'No, I've got to be getting back to Takali. Might be able to grab a lift with somebody. See you around.'

Yeoman re-emerged from the underground operations room adjacent to G Shelter ten minutes later, blinking in the harsh sunlight. The embattled convoy was reported to be somewhere between the islands of Lampedusa and Linosa, with over a hundred miles still to run. Roger Graham's four Spitfires were already out there, making their second trip that morning, and Yeoman had orders to bring his Yellow Section to immediate readiness. He got his pilots together—a sergeant named Randall filling the gap caused by the loss of Wilcox—and they went out to their aircraft, blistering in their pens under the brazen sun.

They waited for twenty minutes, fuming at the delay in the scorching heat, and still no call came for them to scramble. Then, suddenly, they heard the roar of Merlin engines swelling from Takali. Spitfires swung up through the rippling heat haze, tucking up their wheels and climbing out to sea. More came racing up from Hal Far, showing their elliptical wings as they turned over Zurrieq and sped off to the west, climbing hard.

Another five minutes went by, then Yeoman threw his helmet on to the wing of his Spitfire and called out to Powell, in the next pen:

'Bugger this. I'm going back to G Shelter to find out what's going on. Keep an eye on things here; if the flare goes up while I'm away you take over and get airborne. I'll catch up with you.'

He grabbed a bicycle that was propped against the wall of sandbags and mounted it, pedalling off towards G Shelter and cursing because of the amount of sweat it cost him. By the time he arrived he was in no mood to mince words with anyone. Flinging down the bicycle, he stormed down the steps into the ops room and made for the controller, a squadron leader.

'What the blazes is going on?' he demanded.

The controller looked at him coldly. 'Are you talking to me?' he asked.

'Yes, I bloody well am,' Yeoman retorted, still fuming. 'We've been sitting out there roasting for half an hour on readiness, and then we see everybody else getting airborne except us. So what's happening?'

There was a long pause while the squadron leader, his face turning slowly purple, looked Yeoman up and down as though the pilot were something that had just crept out from under a stone. Then he said:

'As a matter of fact, the convoy is now within range of the Takali and Hal Far fighters. They will be providing the air cover from now on.'

'Well,' stormed Yeoman, 'somebody might have bloody well told us. My pilots need all the rest they can get.' He put his face very close to the controller's and said, in a low, level voice:

'Have you any idea what it costs us every time we have to

sit out there waiting for a scramble? No, I don't suppose you have, so I'll tell you. We have our guts in our mouths. We want to relieve ourselves all the time. We feel sick. The longer the wait lasts, the worse it gets. In some ways, it's worse when no scramble comes than when it does. The anticlimax rips you apart, makes you feel washed out. And yet you know that you have to go on doing it, over and over again, your nerves getting more strung up each time. Some can't take it any more, and do away with themselves. You've heard about those cases, haven't you?' He stood with his hands on his hips, feet apart, and glared truculently at the other officer. The squadron leader, a man in his forties who wore an observer's brevet, took a deep breath, stared back at Yeoman and then let out a long sigh, relaxing visibly.

'Let me tell you a couple of things,' he said quietly. 'First, I don't like your tone or your manner, but we'll forget that. Second, yes, I do know what it's like. In the last war I was an observer on RE8s—you may have heard of them. Flying around at five thousand feet over the enemy lines, taking photographs—not exactly the recipe for a long and healthy life. I arrived on the squadron in Flanders in February 1918, and by the end of March there were only three of the original bunch left. I was wounded, otherwise I probably wouldn't be here now. When things were really hectic, we lived on a diet of milk and cognac. We couldn't keep anything else down. So don't go sounding off to me about strain and the like.'

'All right, sir,' Yeoman said, somewhat chastened. 'I went off at half-cock and I apologize.'

'Forget it,' the squadron leader said. 'We're all on edge. Now, I'm going to have to ask you to remain at readiness for another half hour or so; all the Spits we can spare are out looking after the convoy, and Jerry might put over a sneak raid. But I'll stand you down as soon as possible, that I promise you.'

Mollified, and angry with himself because of his impetuosity, Yeoman left the operations room and cycled back to the pens. Powell noticed the expression on his face and was curious.

126

'You look as though you've had a brush with authority,' he said. 'What happened?'

'Oh, I just blew my top and made a silly ass of myself, that's all,' Yeoman replied. 'Anyhow, we have to stay on readiness for another half-hour or so.'

Briefly, he outlined what the controller had told him about the convoy's progress. As it turned out, the squadron leader was correct in his assumption that the enemy would send over a raid while the Takali and Hal Far Spitfires were absent: fifteen minutes later, the alarm went up.

The four Spitfires of Yellow Section, still burdened by their auxiliary tanks, climbed hard into the blue-white dome of the sky. For Yeoman, the sortie was a nightmare; during the climb he was seized by violent stomach cramps, and it took all his will-power to avoid vomiting over himself. Weakly, his head swimming, he called up Group Captain Douglas and asked for instructions. The reply came back immediately:

'Six plus big jobs approaching Gozo, Angels fifteen. Steer three-oh-five.'

There was no report of any fighters. The Spitfires continued their climb, the pilots searching the sky for first sight of the enemy. At eight thousand feet the instrument panel swam in front of Yeoman's eyes and he was having trouble focusing. At ten thousand feet he almost passed out, recovering to find that his Spitfire was in a shallow dive.

Powell's voice came over the radio, full of concern.

'Yellow One, are you in trouble? George, are you okay?'

Fighting off an attack of nausea, Yeoman replied: 'I've had it, Gerry. The Dog. Take over.'

Powell acknowledged and Yeoman turned away, flying instinctively as he turned down towards Luqa. The rubbery smell of his oxygen mask made his gorge rise and he tore it away from his face, opening the cockpit canopy and taking great gulps of the air that rushed in.

Waves of heat and cold swept over him alternately as he began his approach to land, his senses swimming. Automatically he lowered the undercarriage and flaps, fishtailing to lose speed as he sank towards the runway, touching down with a series of jarring bumps. He turned off the runway as the Spitfire slowed, following the winding taxi-track towards his blast pen on the airfield perimeter close by the village of Siggiewi. Stopping beside the sandbags, he hastily undid his straps and fell from the cockpit, disgorging the contents of his stomach into the dust, clinging to the trailing edge of the wing for support. Then, the pain in his stomach like a red-hot knife, he staggered round the pen and managed to drop his shorts in the nick of time.

A few minutes later, feeling a little better, he sat in the shelter of the sandbags and sipped water from a bottle proffered by Sykes. A few miles away, the Takali anti-aircraft barrage was making a thunderous din. Tozer stuck his head over the parapet, shading his eyes against the glare as he peered upwards.

'There they are,' he said, pointing. 'Two . . . four . . . eight of 'em. Junkers 88s. Whoops—' his voice rose excitedly—'there go the Spits!'

Yeoman looked up, his sickness and weariness temporarily forgotten, following the direction of Tozer's outstretched arm. The bombers were turning over the west coast of the island at about twelve thousand feet, flying in two diamond-shaped formations, slipping through layers of flak bursts like silvery fish. Above them, streaking down to intercept, came the three Spitfires, the clarion note of their Merlin engines under full power cutting through the deeper throb of the Junkers' motors.

The Spitfires flashed through the rearmost box of bombers, the popping of their cannon clearly audible, their wings glittering in the sun as they pulled out below and rocketed into a climb in line astern. A Junkers turned lazily out of formation, spiralled twice and then went into a vertical dive, trailing a chalk slash of white smoke from both engines.

The leading box of bombers was nosing over, the silhouettes of the aircraft growing larger.

'It's us,' said Sykes breathlessly. 'Better take cover.'

Yeoman, mentally calculating the bombers' diving angle,

corrected him. 'No, I think it's Valletta again. They'll pass over the top of us.'

He was right. The bombers came on, plunging through the smoke of the shell-bursts from the ack-ack batteries in and around Hamrun, Floriana, Valletta, Sliema, Senglea and Luqa itself, carpeting the sky with such an intensity of fire that the diving aircraft were only briefly visible. Through the murk their bombs fell, shrieking down in a long parabola towards the installations of Grand Harbour.

Before they hit the ground, there was a terrific explosion from the opposite direction. Startled, the three men turned their heads. The stricken Junkers had hit the ground somewhere between Rabat and Luqa with its bombs still on board. Dark clouds of smoke boiled up from the spot, and the thick white trail of its fall rose arrow-straight into the sky like a tombstone.

There were more cracking detonations as the bombs from the other Junkers exploded, and pillars of smoke rose from the Grand Harbour area, forming a line on the horizon. The bombers, having pulled out of their dives, were twisting and turning this way and that through the murderous barrage, seeking the sanctuary of the sea. They appeared to get away unscathed.

Yeoman suddenly remembered the second box of four bombers and looked for it, locating it through the howl of Spitfire engines. The three surviving Ju 88s had passed overhead and were diving on Hal Far, still harassed by the fighters whose pilots were braving the ack-ack from Safi, Kalafrana, Marsaxlokk and Delimara to press home their attacks.

Yeoman watched one Spitfire, clinging to the tail of a bomber like a leech, close right in to a range of only a few yards. White flame flared up from the Junkers' wings; it held its course for a few seconds, then blew up, the shock wave rippling out through the drifting ack-ack bursts and pushing them aside. The pursuing Spitfire flew through the cloud of smoke and debris and Yeoman saw it turn away, descending steeply towards Safi.

The remaining bombers, with the other Spitfires in hot pursuit, dropped their bombs almost at random and jinked away over the sea. After a while, the Spits gave up the chase and came back to Luqa, landing and taxiing in. The returning pilots were Powell and Randall, and the former came up to Yeoman with the news that Kearney had landed safely at Safi. The Irishman, Powell announced in a tone of disgust, had accounted for both the 88s destroyed.

'Couldn't get a look in for the bugger,' he said. 'The boy sure can fly. Thought he'd bought it, though, when I saw him disappear smack through the middle of what was left of his second Hun.'

A few minutes later, two Spitfires appeared in the circuit over Luqa. They were the fighters which had set out with Roger Graham earlier that morning to fly top cover over the convoy. Their exhausted pilots told how they had become involved in a hell of a scrap with Junkers 87s and swarms of Messerschmitt 109s just at the point where they were about to turn for home. Graham and his number two had both been shot down in flames, and there was no hope that either of them could have survived.

Throughout the day, the sky over Malta echoed with the crackle of Merlin engines as the Spitfires went out again and again to protect the remnants of the convoy. Returning pilots, sweat-soaked and exhausted, brought back stories of terrific air battles over the sea, always against vastly superior numbers. They tore great gaps in the enemy's ranks, but they suffered heavily themselves, too; by the end of the day, losses in combat and battle damage had halved the strength of every fighter squadron on the island.

That evening, two freighters—the sole survivors of the six which had left Gibraltar four days earlier, their hulls blackened and scarred by near misses, pock-marked by splinters —limped into the shelter of the Grand Harbour. One of the freighters was badly damaged; a bomb had torn a great gap in her side and one of her holds was flooded, ruining a quarter of her precious cargo.

Two destroyers, one British, the other Polish, their blast-swept decks crammed with survivors from the ships that had gone down, shepherded the freighters to safety. As they approached the entrance to Grand Harbour, the Polish warship struck a mine and blew up, sinking in a matter of minutes. There were few survivors; those who were rescued were numbed by this cruel twist of fate, scarcely able to believe that their comrades, with whom they had battled through so many dangers, had died within sight of sanctuary.

During the next two days the enemy made determined attempts to sink the merchantmen before their supplies could be unloaded, but each attack was frustrated by patrolling Spitfires and the ack-ack barrage. Yeoman took no part in the air fighting, for the medical officer at Luqa had taken one look at him and ordered him to the military hospital in Umtarfa for a thorough check-up, after which he had been sent to Palestrina House in St. Paul's Bay, the pilots' rest camp.

Powell came to visit him, bringing him grim news of the devastation around Grand Harbour and of friends whose faces they would see no more.

By the morning of Wednesday, 17 June, the last supplies had been unloaded from the freighters. They had been bought with the life-blood of brave men, whose sacrifice would sustain the garrison and people of Malta for just six more weeks.

Chapter Nine

The pilots of No. 2 Squadron, Fighter Wing 66, were playing Skat in the readiness tent. The game had been going on at intervals for a fortnight; a pilot would go off on a mission, and on his return take up more or less where he had left off. If he didn't come back, his stake money went straight into the pot.

Joachim Richter had a handful of spades, and was wondering how to dispose of them, when a breathless runner arrived from base HQ.

'Everybody is to report immediately to the Group Commander's tent,' he announced. 'It's a big circus today.'

Richter laid his hand face-down on the blanket that served as a card table and joined in the general scramble as the pilots searched for their gear. The air was blue with curses.

The squadron truck screeched to a stop outside. 'Come on, for Christ's sake get a move on,' Richter called impatiently, almost tripping over Ernst Sommer, who was grovelling on his hands and knees, trying to retrieve his helmet from beneath a pile of parachute bags which someone had dropped haphazardly in a corner.

They all got themselves sorted out at last and piled on to the truck, which careered away over the field. Richter saw that No. 1 Squadron's transport was also heading in the same direction; as the runner had indicated, something big was in the wind. It was unusual for both squadrons to go out on a mission at the same time; one of them was usually held in reserve.

He hoped it would not be anything too strenuous. Today, 5 July, was Willi Christiansen's birthday, and a celebration was planned for that evening. It promised to be quite a party; a bevy of nurses was coming down from the hospital in Catania, and the pilots were looking forward to some action.

The Wing Commander, Lieutenant-Colonel Dollmann, was waiting for them in his tent, seated behind a trestle table. This was the man who had taken over the Wing after the loss of Colonel Becker, and although he was capable enough he was by no means the leader his predecessor had been. He had spent most of the war so far stationed in Norway, and apart from some skirmishing with the Russians in the far north he had seen very little action. In fact, most of the pilots under his command were more experienced than he was. He was a heavy-featured man, tending to run to fat, even though he was only in his early thirties. He was balding, and when he addressed someone he had the most annoying habit of staring over one's head. He had become firm friends with the base commander, Colonel Dessauer, and most of the pilots thought that they were admirably suited to one another.

Dollmann wasted no time on preliminaries. As soon as all the pilots were gathered around him in a semicircle, he said:

'Gentlemen, today the whole of the Axis air strength in Sicily is to begin phase three of our air offensive against Malta. Our orders, received late last night directly from Commander-in-Chief South, are quite specific. During the next three weeks, we are to destroy every fighter aircraft available to the enemy and are to prevent reinforcements or supplies from reaching the island.'

Richter glanced at Johnny Schumacher and raised an eyebrow. That could mean only one thing: the long-awaited invasion of Malta was coming, and soon.

Dollmann cleared his throat and shuffled some papers that lay before him on the table. 'During the coming phase of the offensive,' he continued, 'our bombers will be concentrating on airfield attacks. We, in addition to our normal escort role, will carry out an increased number of fighter sweeps over these objectives in between the bombing raids, with the object of catching the enemy fighters on the ground while they refuel and re-arm.'

He glanced at his watch. 'Beginning at noon today,' he said, 'one hundred bombers will operate over Malta in relays at ten-minute intervals. Each relay will consist of approximately ten aircraft escorted by twice as many Messerschmitts. This means that in order to sustain the pressure, you will have to fly four, maybe five sorties over the island in the course of the day.

'During today's operations, the bomber escort will be mounted by Fighter Wings 3 and 53. We shall undertake the ground-attack work, timing our strikes to follow every third raid. I emphasize, gentlemen, that accurate timing is absolutely essential. We must not give the Tommies a moment's respite. Our sole purpose is to bring them to battle in the air and to harass them on the ground to the point where operations become impossible for them.'

He went on to give the assembled pilots their take-off times and times over the target. Luqa was to be the primary objective; if this airfield could be neutralized, even temporarily, the surviving Spitfires would be forced to concentrate on Takali and Hal Far and both these objectives could then be attacked in turn. Safi strip, Luqa's satellite landing-ground, had already been badly hit by a high-level Italian air raid earlier that morning, and reconnaissance had indicated that it would probably be out of action for the rest of the day.

Outside Dollmann's tent, after they had been dismissed, Richter gathered the pilots of his No. 2 Squadron around him and had a quiet word with them.

'Look,' he said, taking a pull at his cigarette, 'we all know our feelings about ground attack, especially those of us who were in Russia. So, what I'm saying to you is—no heroics, and that's an order. Go in low and fast, shoot up whatever is directly in front of you and get out. Some of us, the older hands that is, are sometimes tempted to push our luck. We get the feeling we're immune. Well, we are not. Do not, under any circumstances, attempt a second run over the target, even though you don't hit anything on your first pass. If anyone tries it, I'll kick him all the way up Etna and slow-fry his balls over the crater. On second thoughts, I probably won't need to, because he'll be dead anyway. That's all.'

Each of Fighter Wing 66's two squadrons was putting up twelve aircraft. They were to fly in sections of four, each section taking off at twenty-minute intervals. No. 1 Squadron was first away, and by the time it became the turn of the leading elements of Richter's squadron to take off the first two sections of its sister unit had already returned. Richter noticed, grimly, that three Messerschmitts were missing and that several of the others had sustained combat damage. It looked as though a hot reception awaited them.

At twenty past one Richter's pilots climbed into their Messerschmitts. A mechanic, standing on the wing beside the cockpit, helped Richter to fasten his straps and attach his oxygen and radio-telephone leads. The man shouted something, and Richter lifted the flap of his helmet in order to hear better:

'Get one for me, sir!'

The pilot grinned in acknowledgment and operated the switches in the cockpit as the mechanic cranked the handle on the starting-trolley. The Daimler-Benz engine kicked over a few times and then burst into full-throated life. Richter checked the instruments carefully to make sure everything was in order, then waved away the chocks and released the brakes. The Messerschmitt taxied forward, flanked on its right by Hans Weber's aircraft and on its left by Johnny Schumacher's. The fourth 109 of the section, trailing along behind and almost completely obscured by a swirling cloud of dust, was flown by Warrant Officer Buchada.

When they reached the take-off point and swung into wind Buchada drew abreast of the other three; a very necessary precaution, for to take off in the teeth of a cloud of dust, blotting out all forward vision, was to invite disaster.

The pilots opened the throttles and the Messerschmitts

moved forward, their wingtips no more than fifteen feet apart, gathering speed over the bumpy, sandy ground. The rumbling of their wheels ceased abruptly and they were airborne, flashing over the aerodrome perimeter, their shadows flitting over objects which by now had become so familiar: the burnt-out wreck of an Italian Savoia bomber, the skeletal remains of a few trucks, worn out and cannibalized for spare parts.

The Messerschmitts stayed as low as the terrain would permit, speeding over the broad Simeto river that wound its way from the mountains across the plain of Catania. A mile or two to the left, a lake shimmered in the sun; then it was behind them and they were threading their way through the hills and valleys of the Monti Iblei, dotted with numerous white hamlets. Peasants, resting in the shade, looked up as the fighters thundered overhead; in one village a patient donkey, terrified by the sudden crescendo of sound, took flight down the twisting street, scattering its load in all directions.

They followed the line of the little river Irminio and sped over Ragusa, perched on its ridge between two deep gorges. Three minutes later they were over the sea, heading out into the Malta Channel on a heading of two hundred degrees and at a height of not more than a hundred and fifty feet. The course would take them past the north-west tip of Gozo, after which they would turn on to a hundred and seventy degrees for three more minutes before turning sharply eastwards. Then they would leap over Dingli cliffs, make one fast run over Luqa and carry on at low level across the island, finally heading out to sea once more over St. Paul's Bay.

The first leg of the flight was accomplished without incident. Gozo slid by, well over on the left, and the fighters turned south-south-east on their second heading, the pilots alert for any sign of danger.

As they turned towards Malta, they could see a great deal of smoke and dust over the island, kicked up by the explosions of bombs. A few thousand feet higher up, drifting slowly on the wind, a host of flak-bursts had mingled to form another, thinner smoke layer.

The white slash of Dingli cliffs leaped towards them. So far, there was no sign of any other aircraft, either enemy or friendly. Knowing exactly where Luqa lay beyond the cliffs, Richter turned slightly more to the right; the other three Messerschmitts accompanied him effortlessly, as though held to him by an invisible thread.

A slight back pressure on the control column took the fighters leaping over the cliffs, and the whole panorama of the island lay before them. Richter took in the whole scene with one swift glance, and realized at once that their timing was near perfect. A raid had just ended, and over the northern end of the island clusters of new anti-aircraft bursts betrayed the position of the retreating bombers. The bombers themselves were invisible, as were any fighters that might have been pursuing them, but looking ahead Richter saw something that brought elation welling up inside him; several Spitfires were in the Luqa circuit, their wheels and flaps down as they prepared to land.

For the first time since they had taken off, Richter broke radio silence. 'Spitfires over Luqa,' he warned the others. 'Remember, straight in and straight out again.'

The circling Spitfires would be low on fuel and doubtless out of ammunition. It was a heaven-sent opportunity to knock a few down without fear of pursuit.

It took the speeding Messerschmitts forty-five seconds to cover the four miles between Dingli and Luqa. They flashed over Siggiewi and the blast pens on that part of the airfield perimeter, but Richter had no time to note whether there was anything in them or not because at that instant a Spitfire loomed up in front of him. Its pilot appeared to have seen the danger, because he made a desperate attempt to escape at the last moment, starting to retract his undercarriage and climbing. He was too late. Richter pressed both triggers on his control column, sending a lethal burst of 7.9-mm machine-gun bullets and 20-mm cannon shells into the British fighter just forward of the cockpit. Instantly, a great gush of flame burst from the Spitfire, enveloping the whole of the centre fuselage. The fighter, one undercarriage leg dangling, went into a steep diving turn and ploughed into the ground, bursting apart in boiling gouts of fire.

Richter streaked over the remains, conscious of the other Messerschmitts fanning out and firing at other targets on either side of him. A group of steel-helmeted figures swept into his field of vision, running for their lives, and he instinctively pressed the triggers again, seeing the ground around them erupt in fountains of dust. He did not see whether he had hit any of them. Slightly off to the right he saw what looked like a Wellington, parked half in and half out of a blast pen, and kicked the rudder bar to bring his sights to bear, forgetting about Hans Weber and almost colliding with his number two in the process. They both fired at the Wellington at the same moment, seeing their bullets and shells ripple across the bomber's rear fuselage and tail and kick up sand from the bags around it.

Then they were over and away, speeding over the network of stone walls that lay between Zebbug and Hamrun. Behind them, belatedly and uselessly, the flak opened up, adding to the confusion that already reigned over the airfield.

They raced out over St. Paul's Bay, keeping low until they were clear of the land, then began to climb, turning left until they were flying parallel with the north-east coast of Gozo on a heading that would bring them back to Sicily. Richter called up the others, asking each in turn if he was unharmed; all three replied in the affirmative. Their voices were jubilant; they had destroyed three Spitfires for certain and shot up several more on the ground. If they kept up this sort of pace, the Tommies would soon have no fighters left.

To the hard-pressed garrison on Malta, the shattering series of air attacks in the high summer of 1942 would always be known as the July Blitz. It began on the fifth of the month and ended on the twenty-ninth. In between those dates, the island, and particularly the airfields, reeled under an unprecedented weight of high explosive by day and night. For the exhausted fighter pilots, their numbers dwindling constantly, there was no respite, for almost every daylight raid was followed by a fast hit-and-run attack by Messerschmitts. The spectre of the Dog was always present, its deprivations adding to those of continual air combat, and young men in their prime wasted away until they were haunted shadows of their former selves. The daily diet was atrocious, but nevertheless the best that could be offered on an island under real threat of starvation; a typical lunch consisted of a few shrivelled olives, four ounces of bread, a slice of fried bully beef, three dried figs for dessert and a mug of tea. There were also, when available, two tablespoonsful of shredded carrots soaked in cod-liver oil and one sulphur pill per day, the former nauseating to rebellious stomachs and the latter completely ineffective against dysentery.

Yeoman entered the grim days of the July Blitz fresher and more relaxed than most, thanks to his spell in the pilots' rest camp. Lucia had visited him there, almost every day, and through her eyes he had learned to appreciate new beauty; the glory of the pink haze that crept over St. Paul's Bay with each sunrise, the silver-grey of the olives and deep green of the carob trees on the hillsides, the red earth. Together, they had found beauty even in the barren rocks, speckled with clusters of narcissi and the glowing colours of the flowering prickly pear. In the three days immediately before his return to duty, while he regained much of his lost strength, she had shown him much of the true, ancient Malta, the Malta of the legends, a world removed from the ugly sprawl of Valletta. They had looked down on Ghajn Razul, the 'Spring of the Prophet', where it was said St. Paul had slaked his thirst after being shipwrecked on the island's shores; they had climbed the steep incline overlooking the bay to the little hamlet of Wardija where, Lucia said, wild flowers emerged in a mass of colour all around in the spring and autumn, and afterwards they had walked hand-in-hand down to the fertile valley of Pwales, connecting St. Paul's Bay to Ghajn Tuffieha, the 'Well of Apples'. In a little grotto halfway down the valley Lucia had knelt in simple prayer before a shrine of the

Virgin, and her companion, anxious to please, had knelt beside her. Later, they had climbed the flat-topped hill called Il Qala, opposite the grotto, to look at a series of holes that might have been Phoenician tombs, and then had gone down to the valley again to sit and watch the birds, Lucia laughing as she tried to teach Yeoman to pronounce their names. He learned, and never forgot, that the common-or-garden little house sparrow rejoiced under the name of *ghasfur-il-beit*, or 'roof bird,' and that the ousel was called *tas-sidrija-bajda,* 'white waistcoat'.

On his last day they had walked north from St. Paul's Bay to Mistra, and from there had ascended the dizzy, winding road to Mellieha. There, standing beside the Chapel of Our Lady of Mellieha, they had looked out in silence over the great sweep of Mellieha Bay, and Lucia had quietly told Yeoman the poignant tale of a young woman, the greatest beauty on the island, who had lived near here. They had called her Il Warda Bajda, the White Rose, and artists from far and wide had visited Mellieha, clamouring to paint her portrait. She had always refused, being a modest, retiring girl, and when she died at a tragically early age her beauty had passed into legend.

There had been a strange, unreal quality about those hours spent with Lucia, as though they had been on a different plane, even though the throb of engines and the wail of plummeting aircraft had never been far away. Yeoman had never made any advances to her, and physical contact had been limited to holding hands and the resting of her head on his shoulder as they sat together, and yet he felt somehow fulfilled. It was as though, somehow, to have gone further would have been to risk destroying something precious.

Now, back in action, he had reconciled himself to the fact that he would never see Lucia again. He had come to terms with the inevitability of being killed, knew in his heart that nothing short of a miracle would assure his survival. If death awaited him, he thought, then let it be so; and if there was time for last thoughts and images, then let them be of the pure, unsullied things that had brought him to oases of peace and joy amid the carnage and misery.

His diary, the entries becoming shorter and more laconic, reinforced his belief that he would not come through. He stared at its dog-eared, tea-stained pages now, weary at the end of a day's intensive flying, and mentally ticked off the roll of the dead.

5 July. Luqa hit again and again. Surprise attack on field by 109s. Three Spits shot down while landing. Kearney and one other pilot killed, third pilot badly burned. Squadron moved to Takali and continued operations; down to five serviceable aircraft. Two enemy aircraft destroyed, Takali Spits got five. Two heavy raids on Valletta during night.

6 July. Two sections scrambled at 0800 to intercept raid at 22,000 ft over Gozo. Encountered three Cant bombers and about thirty fighters. Went headlong through the fighters and attacked the bombers, which unloaded their bombs in the sea and turned for home. Fighters came down on top of us and there was a big fight. Shot a Macchi 202 off Powell's tail; went straight down into the sea, a flamer. Confirmed by one of Takali pilots. One more 202 damaged by Al Winter. Scrambled again later that afternoon, Italians again. Self, Powell, Randall, Winter. One Cant destroyed by Powell, one damaged by me. Winter hit by 109s, parachuted and came down in sea, but dead when picked up. Might have been machine-gunned while in water. Scrambled a third time early evening; self, Randall, Powell, Larry Taylor. Intercepted two Ju 88s plus twenty 109s. Taylor hit one bomber, which turned for Sicily flying low over the water and leaving a long trail of white smoke. Randall got the other 88 and a 109, the lucky bastard! I fired at two 109s, but observed no result.

July 8. Taking things easy yesterday, just one or two tip-and-runs by 109s. Everybody patching things up like mad. Workshops at Takali going flat out, practically rebuilding Spits from bits and pieces. Moved back to Luqa in the evening; just as well, because Jerry came back this morning, knocking hell out of Takali. We were able to put up eight Spits (sheer joy!) on first scramble of the day. Scramble call came rather late, with result that Jerry was over the island at 20,000 ft while we were still on our way upstairs to meet him. Couldn't get through to the bombers—six Ju 88s—which dive-bombed Takali right on the nose, but the 109s came piling down on us and we tangled. They chased us all over the bloody airfield. We were so busy watching our tails that we had no chance to pick a target. Randall shot down and slightly injured, but pronounced fit to continue flying.

Second scramble of the day got off to a better start. Seven Spits airborne; self (now officially leading squadron), Powell, Randall, Taylor, Schuyler (South African), Brett and Calder. We were at 22,000 ft when the Ju 88s came in, about 7,000 ft lower down. We went down on them vertically, the airspeed practically off the clock, straight through the screen of fighters. I selected a Ju 88 on the port flank of their formation, levelled out and got in a very fast deflection shot. Miracle! His starboard engine burst into flames. No time to observe further results, because half a dozen 109s swarmed all over me. Kept on turning hard and one of them appeared in front. Hit him in the wing root and he exploded. Did not see him crash, but he was confirmed later by a RMA battery.

While the rest of us tangled with the 109s, Schuyler, Brett and Calder went after the bombers. It seems they failed to see fifteen or twenty more 109s coming from upstairs. Schuyler and Brett were shot down almost immediately and both killed. Calder had a bullet through the thigh and force-landed on Safi. One more 109 destroyed (by Gerry Powell). Not good arithmetic.

And so it had gone on, day after day, the high drama captured in Yeoman's hastily-scrawled sentences. A stranger, reading them, would see only a day-to-day record of sorties, kills and losses, with a few names thrown in, and Yeoman was desperately sorry that there had been no time to write a fuller account, with all those vivid personal glimpses that had gone into these hateful, glorious weeks. Yet there were some aspects which no words could ever capture: the stomach-turning fear one felt, for example, as one frantically tried to land with an aircraft full of holes and half an aileron shot away, with fuel almost exhausted and a sky full of 109s, or the time-stopping terror that accompanied the hellish shriek of a falling stick of bombs, when one tore one's fingers bloody clawing at the hard earth. And it had happened not just once, but time after time.

Neither could words, however expertly phrased, capture the loathing and horror he had felt when, in Rabat, he had come upon a crowd of children—yes, and adults too—hurling stones at something unseen. Forcing his way through the crowd, he had discovered the object of their hatred: an Italian airman, his parachute partly open, impaled on a set of iron railings. The man had still been alive, that had been the worst of it. Then there had been the Spitfire from Hal Far, shot down in mistake by Luqa's guns, impacting on the airfield perimeter and breaking apart. The pilot had been thrown clear, but one arm and both his legs were gone. Yeoman had been one of the first on the scene and had held the boy's head, drenched in his blood, helplessly listening to his animal screams until they faded and then mercifully stopped altogether.

Yeoman wondered how long they could go on. After three weeks of continual action, during which his personal score of enemy aircraft destroyed over Malta had risen to eight —bringing his overall total up to twenty-one—the island's fighter defences had been all but wiped out. Luqa could muster four Spitfires, Takali perhaps five, and Hal Far two. Half a dozen more were repairable, but it would be three or four days before they were returned to the squadrons. Stocks of fuel and ammunition, too, were once again perilously low. As far as pilots were concerned, perhaps half those who had already been on Malta when Yeoman arrived, or who had flown in at the same time, were still alive. Even Hazell, Takali's redoubtable wing commander, who had briefed them on the first evening, had died—machine-gunned, ironically, as he dangled under his parachute.

Most of the others had been forced to bale out once or more; Yeoman and Powell were among the few who had not yet taken to their parachutes. It could only be a question of time before their luck finally ran out.

The four Spitfires climbed in an unreal silence, poised midway between sea and sky, every detail frozen except for the shimmering arcs of their propellers. It was as though time had stood still; only the deep, calm voice of Group Captain Douglas was a link with the living world.

'Ten plus big jobs, Angels twenty, approaching Gozo. Vector three-three-zero.'

And a minute later: 'Thirty plus little jobs, Angels two-five, Gozo, heading one-seven zero.'

Oh, God, would it never end?

'Fifteen plus big jobs and twenty plus little jobs, Angels one-five, north-east of Gozo, heading one-nine-zero.'

Behind Yeoman's four aircraft, the five Spits from Luqa and the pair from Hal Far were also climbing hard. Eleven against seventy-five. Long odds, even for Malta.

Yeoman looked quickly behind. Powell was there, his faithful wingman, with Randall and Taylor a couple of hundred yards astern. His gaze switched to the sky ahead, searching. So far, there was nothing.

'Hello Douggie, George here, still looking.'

'Roger, George. Hold your heading. Bandits ten miles, closing.'

Yeoman pushed a finger under his oxygen mask, scratching an itchy spot among the stubble on his cheek. He had not shaved that morning, because there had been no water to spare for shaving, and even if there had been everybody had run out of razor blades. Leaning forward in his straps, he switched on his reflector sight and turned up the illumination a little; then he moved his gun button from 'safe' to 'fire'.

Strangely, the simple action had a relaxing effect on him. His hands and feet moved automatically on the controls while his mind, seemingly detached from the rest of him, assumed a keenness and alertness such as he had not experienced for a long time.

His altimeter showed twenty-four thousand feet and he levelled out, easing back the throttle a little. He was puzzled; if the first enemy formation was where it ought to be, the ack-ack batteries on Gozo should be pointing the way by now, but the sky was empty. He searched all around once more, dropping each wing in turn to clear the Spitfire's blind spot, but still there was nothing. He pressed the R/T button and called up Douglas again.

'Hello Douggie, George here, still looking. Instructions?'

The calm voice came back immediately. 'Roger, George. You should be fishing. I repeat, you should be fishing. Over.'

Douglas was telling him that the Spitfires were very close to the enemy. He searched the sky again, very carefully, making sure that he had covered every quarter.

At first he thought it was an illusion, a trick of vision. He blinked and looked again. This time, there was no doubt. Several thousand feet below, crawling across the grey green backdrop of Gozo, were the distinctive shapes of a dozen Junkers 88s, their camouflage blending perfectly with the ground far below. Only the glint of sun on a cockpit canopy had revealed their position.

There was time for a quick call to control. 'We're fishing, Douggie. Out.' Then, to the other pilots: 'Tango Red, Tango Red, bandits ten o'clock low. Stand by.'

He made a last search of the dangerous sky, above, behind and to either side, and saw nothing of the escorting Messerschmitts. They must be around somewhere, but he would have to take the risk.

'Tango Red, Tango Red, one, two, three, go!'

He pushed over the stick, rolling the Spitfire on its back, then pulled the stick into his stomach so that the fighter plummeted down in a powerful dive towards the bombers. The other Spits were with him, following him down. They were over the northern tip of Malta now, and the first of the flak was starting to come up, the bursts a long way below the bombers.

The Spitfires swept down on the Junkers formation like arrows. Yeoman leveled out a few hundred yards astern of the right-hand bomber, giving himself a straight no-deflection shot. The 88's wingspan grew until its tips touched the edges of his gunsight ring. Tracer fleeted over his cockpit, but he ignored it.

The Spitfire juddered as he pressed the gun button. The grey trails of smoke from his wings converged on the bomber's port engine, crept across the fuselage centre-section, past the rear gunner's position, and found the engine on the other side. Metal plates broke away from it and it began to smoke, disgorging intermittent puffs that quickly became a thickening stream.

The bomber's outline, shrouded in smoke now, was enormous, filling the whole sky. Yeoman pulled back the stick, feeling an instant of wild panic, believing that a collision was inevitable, then he was shooting over the top of the smoking mass and rolling away, looking back to see the Junkers going down with white flames bursting from its wings.

Five thousand feet higher up, Lieutenant Hans Weber was the first of the escorting Messerschmitt pilots to notice that the bombers were in trouble. He shouted a warning over the radio and Richter, cursing, brought the two squadrons of Fighter Wing 66 down like an avalanche in pursuit of the harrying Spitfires. How the latter had escaped his attention so far was beyond him, for the Messerschmitts had been weaving ceaselessly over their charges for some minutes, but there was no time to worry about it now. Taking in the situation at a glance, he saw that one Junkers was already falling in flames and another was trailing smoke. There was no time to be lost.

Gerry Powell, intent on chopping a Ju 88 to pieces, never saw the plunging Messerschmitts until it was too late. A burst of tracer, snickering over his wings, warned him of the danger and he hauled the stick into his stomach with a wrench that threatened to tear it out of its socket, pulling round in a tight turn to face the danger.

They were coming at him from every quarter. He kept on turning, his breath coming in strangled gasps with the effort. Oh, Christ, they were everywhere, black crosses, mottled camouflage, twinkling cannon. He knew that he must not change direction, that he had to go on turning.

He sensed a terrific blow. It seemed a long way away, happening to someone else. There was an instant, an eternity of drifting, and encompassed within it was all the love and hate, the joy and pain he had experienced in his young life. The letter he had started to write to his girl, back in Peace River, and never finished. If only he had finished it. Then she would have known. Then she would have understood. And then—

Nothing.

Turning clear of the bombers, Yeoman saw a Messerschmitt pull out of its dive, climbing hard. He opened the throttle, clawing for height, for the pursuit of the bombers had taken him down to ten thousand feet. He looked round, forcing himself to stay calm, trying to locate the other Spitfires, and for a split second caught a glimpse of something far below, a seagull, spiralling towards the water, its wings white in the sun. But it wasn't a seagull, it was Powell's Spitfire, and in that same moment Yeoman knew that he had lost his friend.

The instinct of self-preservation, for the moment, pushed all other sentiment from his mind. He twisted in his straps, searching, but although the enemy must be there he could not see them.

The Messerschmitt he had spotted a few seconds earlier was still climbing, weaving a little from side to side. Yeoman opened the throttle wide and went after it. It was as though icy water coursed through his veins, turning him into something that was no longer completely human. He was a killing machine, completely at one with the vibrating metal parts of his fighter.

The pilot of the Messerschmitt seemed to be in no hurry. He levelled out and went into a gentle turn, then reversed his direction and flew east, keeping clear of the Takali flak. Yeoman closed on him steadily, following his movements and keeping slightly underneath him, taking advantage of his blind spot.

Hans Weber was both elated and worried. Elated, because the Spitfire he had just shot down was his third kill over Malta; worried, because his radio had packed in and he had lost touch with the rest of the squadron. For the moment he found himself alone in a hostile sky, and was contemplating whether to run for home or continue his search for the others. Surely he must spot them at any moment, as they turned out over the coast. He had experienced this sort of thing before, this feeling of utter solitude in a sky that was known to be filled with aircraft, and it always left him with an uncanny crawling along his spine.

There was no warning. Yeoman's first burst of cannon fire found the 88-gallon petrol tank immediately behind Weber's seat. It was three parts empty, and the exploding shells instantly ignited the volatile fuel vapour. The Messerschmitt broke apart, the explosion tearing off both wings along with the rear fuselage and tail unit. The cockpit and engine, with Weber's pulped body inextricably mingled with the remains of the instrument panel, fell like a stone and impacted a few hundred yards north of the village of Attard, gouging a six-foot-deep crater.

Circling over Salina Bay with the rest of his squadron, Joachim Richter waited to make rendezvous with the bombers and escort them home after their attack. They had driven off the Spitfires, and the British fighters seemed to have vanished.

Suddenly, Richter realized that Hans Weber was no longer

with them. Together with Johnny Schumacher, he detached himself from the rest of the formation and dived across the centre of the island between Mosta and Birkirkara, pulling up sharply over Rabat and curving round towards the north-east once more.

As they came out of the turn, Richter saw a lone aircraft several thousand feet above, heading in the same direction as themselves, and felt momentary relief, thinking that it was Weber on his way to rejoin the others. Then the relief died inside him, for the other machine had the distinctive elliptical wing shape of the Spitfire. He called up Schumacher, alerting him, and the two Messerschmitts bounded upwards, their pilots aware that they could outclimb the British fighter.

'We've got this bastard, Johnny,' Richter said. 'You take him. He's all yours.'

Their intended victim, meanwhile, had sighted the Ju 88 formation, crawling across the sky over St. George's Bay after bombing Valletta, and was determined to cut it off before it got too far out to sea. The other members of his squadron had been scattered all over the sky after the short, sharp battle that had cost Powell his life, but he had managed to make radio contact with them and they were now racing towards a rendezvous over Mellieha. The Spitfires from Takali were apparently engaged in a fierce fight off Comino with a second incoming enemy formation.

It was an anonymous voice over the radio that saved Yeoman.

'Spit by itself, look out!'

The call might have been intended for anybody but Yeoman reacted to it instinctively, pushing stick and rudder bar and standing his fighter on its side, thin condensation trails streaming from his wingtips as he hauled the Spitfire round in as tight a turn as he had ever made. He saw the two Messerschmitts almost at once, rocketing up to meet him, and in that same instant the leading aircraft opened fire, its tracers passing through the bit of airspace he had occupied only a moment before.

The 109s shot past and he turned in behind them, but more

Messerschmitts were coming up hard on his starboard quarter and he turned towards them instead, seeing them break to the left and right as he held the Spitfire steady, snapping off a shot at one of them but missing by a long way.

It was hopeless. A glance in his rear-view mirror revealed half a dozen enemy fighters spearing down at him, queueing up to shoot him out of the sky. The bastards were sweeping over the island in relays, making sure that the few remaining Spitfires had no chance of taking a real crack at the bombers.

All right, you sods, he thought, you might nail me, but I'll give you a run for your money.

He pushed the Spitfire's nose down and headed flat out for Takali, the nearest airfield. He swept over Rabat at a hundred feet, with three Messerschmitts astern and closing fast. The airfield perimeter swept under him and he stayed low, consciously holding the Spitfire a few feet off the ground, praying that the Bofors gunners were on the ball.

They were. Behind him, between his fighter and the speeding Messerschmitts, the sky over the field became alive with black blotches as the gunners hurled strings of shells at the 109s. One of them, half its tail torn away, hit the ground and bounced upwards in a shower of wreckage, described a graceful parabola over the field and crashed near the sandstone cliffs in a gush of blazing fuel. The others came through the barrage unscathed, but almost immediately the first flak-bursts from the Luqa defences blossomed out in front of them and they broke away, turning across Zebbug to head outwards over the west coast of the island.

Richter looked back as he climbed, with Johnny Schumacher's Messerschmitt sliding into place astern and to the right. Behind them, he could see a tall column of smoke arising from the funeral pyre of the 109 that had crashed on Takali. There would be no birthday party for Willi Christiansen that night, or any other.

Yeoman, circling to the south of Luqa, saw that the sky was suddenly empty. Turning over Kirkop he began his approach to land, lowering undercarriage and flaps, floating over the pock-marked lunar landscape of Safi. He touched down effortlessly, turning aside from the runway towards his blast pen, passing landmarks that were now as familiar to him as the lines on his hands.

He swung the Spitfire round, tail-on to the sandbagged pen, and closed down the engine. The all-clear was sounding as he climbed from the cockpit. Two airmen—strangers to him, not the cheery faces of Sykes and Tozer—came running up to manhandle the fighter into the pen, assisted by a couple of soldiers. He ignored them, walking slowly to the edge of the sandbags, looking out across the field and noticing with tired satisfaction that both Randall and Taylor had got back safely.

But Gerry Powell would not be coming back.

Suddenly, the tension went out of Yeoman and he went completely to pieces, collapsing like a rag doll, falling to his knees behind the sandbags, mercifully sheltered from the eyes of the ground crew. Hating himself for the weakness, ashamed and at the same time relieved, he wept like a child. Between his trembling knees, his tears darkened the parched earth.

Chapter Ten

It was a sultry day, and the windows of the conference room of the Führer's headquarters at Rastenburg were wide open. An electric fan attached to the ceiling hummed quietly, pushing out a faint stream of lukewarm air.

It had been a lengthy conference, with situation reports from the various fronts discussed in detail. Hitler was in a cheerful, almost boisterous mood, with good reason it seemed. On the eastern front, the Russians were withdrawing in the Donets Basin; they had already evacuated Rostov and Novocherkassk.

'Everywhere,' the Führer exclaimed, 'our armies are victorious. Our summer offensive has been an overwhelming success. Sevastopol, thanks largely to the efforts of your Stukas, Richthofen'—he nodded affably at General Wolfram von Richthofen, the commander of VIII Air Corps, whose dive-bombers had smashed a path for the Wehrmacht ever since the first campaigns in Poland—'has fallen at last. Manstein's 11th Army and our Rumanian allies have taken 97,000 prisoners.

'The offensive continues,' Hitler went on, his voice vibrant. 'Field-Marshal List's Army Group A, consisting of Rouff's 17th Army, Kleist's 1st Panzer Army and Constantinescu's 3rd Rumanian Army, is already moving into the western Caucasus, sweeping all resistance aside. Further north, covering this operation, Field-Marshal Weichs' Army Group B—that is to say, Salmuth's 2nd Army, Jany's 2nd

Hungarian Army and Gariboldi's 8th Italian Army—is forming a defensive line along the Don, protecting List's flank, while Paulus's 6th Army is pushing on towards the Volga.' He tapped the map, spread in front of him on the table. 'Paulus's objective is here: the city of Stalingrad.'

Hitler spoke for a good three-quarters of an hour about the latest situation on the Russian front, occasionally throwing questions at the staff officers who were gathered around him. The conduct of the war in the east was his main obsession, and he seemed reluctant to move on to other items on the agenda. At length, however, he turned to Rommel's campaign in North Africa. Here, too, all appeared to be going well; Tobruk had fallen in June and the Panzers had raced on into Egypt. Rommel's armoured spearheads were now probing the British Eighth Army's defensive positions between the Qattara Depression and a village on the coast called El Alamein. The British, disorganized by the speed of Rommel's advance had had no time to form a defensive line in the true sense of the word; the gap between the Qattara Depression and the sea was filled by no more than a series of infantry 'boxes', surrounded by barbed wire and mines and supported by some artillery. Rommel was currently bringing his armour and infantry back up to strength after the battles of the previous weeks; once he had done so, he would launch the offensive that would take Panzer Army Africa into Cairo in triumph.

After dismissing North Africa, Hitler moved on to the question of the air defence of the Reich. In May and June the RAF had carried out three massive night attacks on Cologne, Essen and Bremen, each one involving approximately one thousand bombers. Severe damage had been caused, and only a small percentage of the attackers had been destroyed. Clearly, it was time for a reappraisal of the whole defence system.

A man at the far end of the conference table cleared his throat suddenly, taking advantage of a pause in Hitler's monologue.

'Excuse me, mein Führer,' he said, standing stiffly to attention.

Hitler looked up, an annoyed expression on his face.

'Yes, Student,' he snapped. 'What is it?'

'Mein Führer, forgive me, but we appear to have missed an item on the agenda. The item dealing with Operation Hercules.'

Hitler looked blank. 'Hercules?' he said, as though he had never heard the name before.

The paratroop general looked uncomfortable, sensing the stares of the other officers around the table. They ranged from mildly curious to downright hostile. Nobody seemed to have much time for the paratroops, these days, and no wonder. It was fourteen months since they had undertaken an airborne operation.

'Yes, mein Führer,' Student replied, striving to keep his voice level. 'The planned invasion of Malta.'

'Well,' Hitler said, turning to the map once again, 'what of it?'

'The preparations are complete, mein Führer.' Student was beginning to wonder why he had been summoned to Rastenburg in the first place. Nevertheless, he continued doggedly with his report.

'The British air defences on the island have been virtually wiped out,' he said. 'Marshal Count Cavallero and myself are in complete agreement that now is the time to strike, before the British have a chance to fly in more Spitfires. The plan is ready and our sea and air transport is standing by. We can mount the operation in one week from now, if we receive immediate authorization. We have also assembled sufficient reserves—'

Hitler cut him short with a peremptory wave of the hand. He looked directly at Student and gave a small sigh. Then he said patiently, as though explaining something to a small child:

'Student, it appears you have not been listening to the situation reports. Let me, therefore, reiterate the salient points. One: our armies are pushing on into the Caucasus.

154

Two: Panzer Army Africa will soon be in Cairo. Three: our grand strategy has now changed drastically as a result of these successes.'

Hitler made a grandiose sweeping gesture and then went on, his voice rising triumphantly:

'It is obvious what our strategy must be now! Our forces in Russia must drive on through the Caucasus, turning south along the shores of the Caspian and then rolling on through Persia and Iraq to link up with Rommel in Palestine! Our agents in the Middle East are already at work, fermenting revolt and confusion in readiness for the great combined offensive that will bring the Mediterranean completely into our grasp.'

Hitler's luminous eyes took on a faraway expression. His voice softened, assumed an almost dreamy quality, as though he were entering a trance.

'And after the Mediterranean . . . India. That is our ultimate prize. The whole of the majestic sub-continent, wrested from the hands of the British . . . think of it! A great German Empire, stretching from the Arctic to the Indian Ocean, and perhaps even further. . . .'

He came back to reality with a start and his gaze fixed on the paratroop general once more.

'So you see, Student,' he said, 'Operation Hercules will no longer be necessary. With our domination of the Mediterranean complete, the island of Malta will starve. It will be forced to capitulate without the loss of a single German soldier.'

'But, mein Führer,' Student began, 'there is still the problem of Rommel's supply lines. As long as Malta remains in British hands, there will always be the danger that—'

Hitler silenced him again, his voice taking on an angry undertone.

'Enough, Student! The matter is closed. Malta is no longer of concern to us. Let time take its course. I do not wish to hear another word on the subject.'

Student stood where he was for a few moments, utterly dumbfounded. Then, sweeping together his papers, he begged the Führer's leave to be dismissed, his voice scarcely more than a whisper. Hitler replied with a curt nod.

Student clicked his heels and drew himself up, saluting. Hitler did not trouble to acknowledge. The paratroop general turned and strode from the room, leaving the door open behind him.

Chapter Eleven

Yeoman pressed his face against the window, feeling the coolness on his forehead as he peered into the darkness beyond the port wing of the Hudson bomber. It was probably the last time he would ever see Luqa, and now that the moment had come he felt an infinite sadness.

Yeoman was going home. Behind him, between the metal girders of the fuselage, sat the shadowy forms of his companions; Randall, two pilots from Hal Far whom he did not know, and three soldiers. In a few hours' time they would be in Gibraltar, and the following day, with any luck, back amid the greenery of an English summer.

It was 15 August. Five days earlier, in a desperate, do-or-die attempt to relieve Malta, thirteen freighters and the tanker *Ohio* had passed through the Straits of Gibraltar. To support the convoy, every available warship had been assembled; the escort included the aircraft carriers *Victorious*, *Indomitable* and *Eagle*, the battleships *Nelson* and *Rodney*, three anti-aircraft cruisers and twenty destroyers. Three more cruisers and fourteen destroyers were to make rendezvous with the convoy and escort it through 'Bomb Alley' on the last twenty-four hours of its perilous journey. The convoy included the old carrier *Furious*, which would accompany the main body to a point one hundred and fifty miles west of Malta and fly off thirty-eight desperately-needed Spitfires.

The convoy had sailed into the teeth of fearful odds. On the airfields in Italy and Sardinia the enemy had massed nearly eight hundred aircraft. Across the convoy's route between Gibraltar and Tunisia, twenty enemy submarines were lying in wait. In the Sicilian Channel, a force of Italian cruisers, destroyers and torpedo-boats were lurking, ready to attack under cover of darkness after the main escort had turned away.

HMS *Eagle* was the first to die. In the afternoon of 11 August, torn apart by torpedoes, she slid to the bottom in just eight minutes, taking two hundred of her crew with her.

The convoy had pressed on, subjected to murderous air attacks. Shortly before sunset the old *Furious* flew off her Spitfires and turned back to Gibraltar, her mission accomplished. On Malta, hardened ground crews wept with sheer joy as the fighters slid down out of the darkness, touching down between the gooseneck flares; this time the Messerschmitts would have no chance to wipe them out on the ground.

Only five of the merchantmen reached Malta, yet the supplies they carried were sufficient to sustain the island for three vital months. The tanker *Ohio* also got through with her vital cargo of aviation fuel for the Spitfires and torpedo-bombers. Malta had become alive again, determined and on the offensive, ready to tackle the future with resolve.

No one knew what that future might hold, but there was hope. In North Africa, Erwin Rommel had been held in check and the Commonwealth forces had new leaders; General Alexander had been appointed Commander-in-Chief, and the Eighth Army had a new and dynamic commander too, a wiry, energetic man who did not believe in committing his forces to an offensive unless they enjoyed an overwhelming advantage. His name was General Bernard Montgomery.

The Hudson's engines revved, the yellow tips of the propeller blades inscribing a luminous arc outside Yeoman's window. The aircraft vibrated as the pilot taxied out towards the end of the runway.

Memories flooded through him, chasing one another through his mind. He had been on the island for a little over

158

three months, and somehow it seemed as though he had been there all his life.

He wondered how he would look back on it all, in a few years' time, assuming he survived that long. Would the images be as vivid as they were now, or would they be dulled and blurred with the passage of time? Would Lucia's tears, on the night he had told her that he was leaving, remain sharp in his memory, or would they have become something remote and impersonal, thrust deep into the recess of his subconscious? He felt a pang of regret, hating himself momentarily, for he had promised to write to her, and in his heart he knew that he would not. There could be no promises, no vows. There might not even be any tomorrows; there had been none for Gerry Powell, and so many of the others. Graham . . . McCallum . . . Wilcox . . . Hazell . . . Kearney . . . and all those who, known or unknown, had fought and died in these skies.

The Hudson's engines roared as the pilot opened the throttles and Yeoman tightened his seat belt, feeling the sudden surge of power. The bomber lumbered along the runway and Yeoman, used to the relatively short take-off of fighters, inadvertently clutched the edge of his seat. Then the tail came up, and a few moments later the Hudson was airborne, climbing and turning gently back across the island.

Malta, farewell. Will we, he wondered, stand by your courageous people in years to come as they stood so valiantly by us in our time of desperate need?

The Hudson came out of its turn and steadied on its course, climbing into the western sky. Yeoman craned his neck, looking back into sudden brilliance as the moon emerged from behind a bank of cloud, her rays tracing a path over the sea. And all at once, it was as though the darkened island was surrounded by a ring of phosphorescence, as the moonlight kissed the surf on the rocks and coves around the western shore, from Ras L'Artal to Ghajn Tuffieha.

And this, above all, was the memory he brought home with him, from the George Cross Island.

The end

A SELECTED LIST OF FINE NOVELS
THAT APPEAR IN CORGI

The prices shown below were correct at the time of going to press. (Oct. '81)

ORDER FORM